Entangled
Hearts

A FORBIDDEN JOURNEY OF LOVE

Entangled Hearts

ROBERT A. CROTHERS

Copyright © 2023 by Robert A. Crothers.

All rights reserved. No part of this publication may be reproduced, distributed, or transmitted in any form or by any electronic or mechanical means, including information storage and retrieval systems, without a prior written permission from the publisher, except by reviewers, who may quote brief passages in a review, and certain other noncommercial uses permitted by the copyright law.

Library of Congress Control Number: 2024901620

ISBN:	979-8-89228-051-8	(Paperback)
ISBN:	979-8-89228-052-5	(Hardcover)
ISBN:	979-8-89228-109-6	(eBook)

Printed in the United States of America

Contents

Foreword ix
Dedication xi
Introduction: A Love Story Unfolds xiii

Rebellion and Academic Setback 1
Irrigation Pond Party Fun 7
Earning Money Off-Season 8
Farm Work Promotion 9
Working at D'Amatos 11
The Girl from a Neighboring Towne 13
Beautiful Girl in Car 19
Getting To Know Each Other 22
Our First Date Blue Love Memories 25
Winter Drive-In Romance 28
When we Fell in Love A New Chapter in Life 29
Our Love Story Begins 30
D.W. Fields Park 38
Lincoln Park 39
The Beach The summer of 1967 42
Friendship Ring 46
Return from Vietnam 1972 New Chapter of Life 52
Leaving for Arizona 60
Road trip and New Mexico 61
Desert Love 65
Arriving in Tucson 67
Pam's Invaluable Assistance 70
Finding a Second Job and Exploring Tucson 71
OperationLinebacker II 73

Costly Car Repair Dilemma 76
Pam Seeking Work 78
Job Interview Surprise 80
Finding a New Place to Live 81
Strange Noises in the Night 82
Purchasing New Furniture 84
The Heart-Wrenching Farewell 87
Heartbreaking Goodbye 89
Sad Farewell to Pam 91
Linebacker II Ends 92
Airplane Maintenance and Preparation 100
Wake Island 102
On to Midway 104
Hawaii Bound 107
Strut Surprises: A Crew Chief's Training Tale 113
Vivid Hawaiian Sunset Departure 117
Sunset Symphony 118
Flight Crew Swap Adventure 120
Excited to Return to D-M 122
Second TDY 124
Peanut Butter 129
Buying our First Home 136
Pam's Sudden Departure An Emotional Roller Coaster Ride 141
Living life without You 145
Struggles with Pam's Departure 146
Sergeant Williams Heartfelt Talk 147
Resisting Change: The Temptation at Twilight 149
Sunset Sorrow and Memories 150
A Fresh Start Begins 152
Departure and Depression 154
Suicide attempt 155
Struggles without her 158
Midnight Shift Training Request 161
Dating Again: Henke's Help 165

TV Show Filming Adventure	167
Making changes in my life	171
A Desire for Children Denied	173
Chance Encounter Sparks Connection	175
Church comes back into my Life.	179
Final TDY	181
Return to DM	187
Moving from the 100th to the 355th	194
Military Service or Civilian Life	197
Leaving Tucson	201
Second Chance at Love	202
Love Dilemma Again	209
The Farm	211
The Finding of Pam	218
About the Author	223

Foreword

This autobiographical memoir is a tapestry of experiences, emotions, and moments curated from the intersection of reality and creative storytelling.

In crafting these narratives, great care has been taken to preserve the essence of truth while veiling personal identities. No names have been left untouched; they have been altered or entirely fabricated to honor the privacy and respect the sanctity of personal stories.

This amalgamation of fact and fiction is a deliberate choice within these pages to resonate universally while maintaining the author's right to artistic expression. Each story bears the weight of genuine emotions and experiences, albeit housed within the protective cloak of fictionalized representation.

May you journey through these pages with an open heart and a discerning mind, embracing the rich tapestry of life. Enjoy the immersive narrative that blurs the lines between reality and imagination!

©2023 by Robert A Crothers

Dedication

To Mr. Norman Marchant, the guiding light of my seventh-grade journey. Your unwavering support and dedication ensured I could move forward in my academic path without looking back. You imparted valuable study skills and instilled in me the ability to decipher the intricate web of knowledge. Your willingness to invest that extra time in my education was a blessing, and I will forever be grateful.

You were, without a doubt, a godsend in my life.

Thank you, Mr. Marchant, for being the beacon of guidance and inspiration in my seventh-grade year. Your impact on my life is immeasurable.

Mr. Paul D'Amato, your unwavering faith in me and the second chance you provided when you hired me at your store were life-changing moments. You saw beyond the mistakes of my youth and believed in my ability to transform into an honest, hardworking individual. Your mentorship and strong work ethic instilled in me under your guidance were invaluable. You took a chance on me, and I am forever grateful for that opportunity to prove to you that I have changed since our first meeting. From January 6, 1966 to December 5th,1967 I proudly worked at your store, and it was during that period that I became a better person. Though you are no longer with us, your impact on my life endures, and I carry the lessons you taught me with me to this day.

To all my former crew chiefs and specialists stationed with me at Davis-Monthan with the 100th OMS and the 99th SRW in Thailand from August 1973 to December 1974, thank you for being tolerant of me during that period. I am incredibly grateful to the following who stuck with me during my darkest days at D-M, SMSgt. Williams, MSgt.

Frederick, SSgt Motes, TSgt Henke, and Sgt Miller. To others I may have forgotten, you were there when I needed you and the help you provided to me in overcoming a challenging time was a mind-jolting, eye-opening reality.

To the remarkable woman who breathed new life into my darkest days from October 1973 to December 1974. It was her unwavering presence that made my life worth living again. Her steadfast support and friendship from the beginning of this challenging journey and throughout my time in Tucson provided the strength I needed to move forward. Even though her departure to Germany left an immense void, the cherished memories of our time together continued to light my path as I continued my journey through life.

And to my parents and siblings who had to endure those early years with me as your son and big brother, it's truly an honor to be part of your stronghold.

Introduction
A Love Story Unfolds

In the quiet corners of a small neighboring town in Massachusetts, a love story unfolded that would leave an indelible mark on the heart of its narrator. A tale of young love, chance encounters, and the enduring power of affection. It all began during the tumultuous junior high years when our protagonist was still finding his way through life, a time marked by insecurity and the quest for identity. During this challenging period, an unexpected turn of events set the stage for a story that would shape the course of his life.

As a teenager, he resorted to an act of youthful mischief – a petty theft from the corner store. Little did he know that this act of rebellion would eventually lead him to a place where his life would take an unforeseen turn. When he turned 16, he found himself employed at the very store he had once pilfered from. With a twist of fate, he would be introduced to the love of his life.

She was the embodiment of beauty, with the prettiest brown eyes, an enviable petite figure, and a captivating smile that could light up even the darkest of days. Their love story began in the early days of their youth, a whirlwind of amusement parks, drive-in movies, and sandy beaches. Yet, the most magical chapter of their story was penned one winter in a place that felt like it had been plucked straight out of a fairy tale – Edaville Railroad.

Edaville Railroad was a place where dreams come true, where an old steam train would gently pull them through cranberry bogs adorned with a myriad of colored lights. Our protagonist fell hopelessly in love with the brown-haired beauty by his side amid the enchanting glow of those lights.

But love, as beautiful as it can be, is not without its complications. Jealousy reared its ugly head, casting a shadow on their romance. It was the day he gave her a friendship ring that marked the beginning of their parting, a decision fueled by his insecurities.

Fast forward four years, his life has taken a different turn. Our protagonist had embarked on a second tour in Vietnam, and on his return, the love he had lost had matured into something different. She followed him to Arizona, where he was stationed for four years. However, their happiness would be short-lived as rumors of infidelity swirled around him while he was overseas. The truth, however, was far from the rumors, as he had almost lost his life in the line of duty.

With her departure, our protagonist found himself struggling through three long years without her. Then, a phone call one evening in August of 1976 changed everything. She had reached out to him, and at that moment, he decided to leave Arizona and return to Massachusetts, where their paths would cross once more.

But as life would have it, the reunion was marked by a new player entering the scene. Our protagonist was faced with a difficult decision, one that would test the depth of his love and the strength of his resolve. In the pages that follow, the story unfolds, painting a vivid picture of love, loss, and the resilience of the human heart as he makes a life-altering choice, one that would carry profound consequences.

This is a story of love's enduring power, the choices we make, and the profound impact they have on the tapestry of our lives. Join us on this journey as we delve into the depths of this captivating love story, where the complexities of the human heart are laid bare and where the pages of life turn to reveal the many facets of affection.

Rebellion and Academic Setback

In June 1962, I experienced an unexpected shift from sixth grade to seventh grade. My problem was provisional; if I couldn't meet seventh-grade expectations, I'd be swiftly returned to my previous sixth-grade class.

My parents believed I needed to channel more dedication into my studies. Consequently, they took away what meant the most to me: my beloved trumpet. Its absence also meant I was forbidden from participating in the junior high band during the initial year.

In response, rebellion became my primary coping mechanism. My life aspirations took a sharp turn. I aspired to become one of the local truant kids, cultivating a reputation as a bad boy and troublemaker akin to the allure of James Dean.

I approached a group leader with whom I was familiar and expressed my interest in joining their group. Instead of a warm reception, he dismissively laughed at my request before turning to face me. He explained that my inclusion wasn't solely up to him and that others needed to decide if I would be a good fit for the club. A meeting was arranged, and a formal vote was taken regarding my membership. To my shock, the final test they proposed was for me to pilfer snacks from a local supermarket, an initiation they deemed necessary to prove my worthiness to join their ranks.

We had several supermarkets in towne. But the two I focused on were Gates Supermarket and D'Amatos. They were close to where I had to go with the stolen snacks. I thought for a while and then went to Gates market first. As I walked the snack aisle, I realized it would be too easy for them to catch me as the aisles were short and the market was small.

Then, as I turned from the aisle, I ran into my neighbor, Mrs. Lambert. She asked what I was doing and if I wanted a ride home. I reached in on the shelf and took a package of snowballs, the one snack I really didn't like, but I was frazzled by her seeing me there. I told her I was just getting a snack and would be meeting someone and I don't need a ride.. I then proceeded to the register to pay for my purchase. Luckily, I had enough money to cover the fifteen cents it cost. I left the store and headed to D'Amatos. It was a much larger supermarket with long aisles. I tore off the marshmallow coconut covering from my snowball along the way. I threw the covering away and ate the cake portion of the snowball.

And so it was that I would go to D'Amato's supermarket the day before the meeting, where I will steal those snacks to bring to the club's leader's home. One late afternoon, it was quiet and there were few shoppers. I entered the store then proceeded to the snacks aisle. Standing before a trilogy of snacks, I grabbed cupcakes, fruit pies, and sugary snacks off the shelf. I crammed them into my oversized winter coat. The coat I wore was given to me as a coat I was supposed to grow into. But today, it made an excellent place to hide the items I was stealing. So I thought!

While committing this crime, I did not realize that one of the store managers was watching me. I just missed to check that row of tinted mirror windows toward the back of the store. Behind those casements sat one of the managers, just watching me.

Soon, I felt a hand placed on my shoulder. I continued taking more items and putting them into my coat's pocket. When I turned to look, I saw that it was Paul, one of the store managers. Paul was the youngest of the brothers who had taken over the store's operations since their parents' retirement. His hand started clinching my left shoulder, and as it did, I heard him ask me, '*Who is going to pay for all those snacks I had just watched you stored it in your coat's pocket.*' Then he asked, '*Did you intend to just walk out of here and not pay them?*' I said, 'No, sir,' and told him, '*My mother was at the back checkout register waiting for me,*' thinking he would never question that and just let me go. Not Paul! His hand firmly grasping my shoulder now and taking control, he guided me to the back register, where the only person there was Mrs. Rodgers, the clerk. I knew Mrs. Rodgers, as her daughter, was a classmate of mine. I was in trouble when I saw her; no one was in line at the register. Paul asked her if my mother was through the register? When Mrs. Rodgers said no, Paul quickly turned me around, and we returned to the aisle we had just left. He told me to remove all the snacks I had taken from his shelves and return them to the same rack as I found them. Then, he pointed the store's entrance door. And being somewhat nice about this incident, he asked me to never set foot into this store again.

After that incident in D'Amatos, I realized that getting in trouble, the possibility of spending time sitting in a police station, or, worse yet, having my father find out about my stealing was not what I needed. I knew I had to straighten my life out.

I began spending more time alone. I spent long hours riding my bike to other townes and out to the ballfields, where I pictured myself playing in the major leagues. Then, one day, while I rode my bike from my grandmother's house in Hanover, I passed this store in the Rockland strip mall. I saw these small cars on an oval track painted on their windows. As I entered the store, I was drawn to the numerous oval tables where kids stood and small cars racing around. I could hear those standing to the side of the oval cheering their vehicles on. Some cars overtake others. I continue to watch with intent. It was evident that slot cars were evolving into a popular pastime.

After completing the 7th grade, with the help of my seventh-grade science teacher, Mr. Marchant, I was promoted to the 8th grade. One of Mr. Marchant's motivating moves was when he gave me detention. In the detention room, he had me sit at a desk and look at the clock on the wall. My detention was only fifteen minutes as I was a bus rider, and they would not keep me from missing the bus. As I sat there, he told me to start counting the seconds as part of my detention. Counting those seconds made it seem those fifteen minutes were hours. I took what he taught me that day in detention, and when the Air Force sent me to survival school, I used that detention while I was placed in the tiger box. It was my most prolonged detention during my junior high school year. It would also be the only detention I would have with Mr. Marchant.

Because of the help I received from Mr. Marchant in being promoted, my parents allowed me to be part of the band. I met this kid in the band who played saxophone, Paul. As we became friends, I asked him if he liked slot cars. Paul, my bandmate, helped me learn and better understand the electric motors and the slot cars' body and what I could do to improve the car for racing. Being a part of this new fad, slot cars racing, was something I thought was *'wicked cool.'* And my new friend, Paul, and I became close. We grew to enjoy the new fad of slot cars. We remained close friends until the end of high school. Having Paul as my new friend and our love of slot car racing helped turn my junior high school years around.

To enjoy the new sport of slot cars racing, I needed money. First, in the summer of 1963, I started mowing lawns. In the winter of that year, I began to sell my services of shoveling snow from neighbors' driveways and sidewalks. Then I tried my hand at recycling newspapers. Which would fail, as it required help from my parents to allow me to have them help me with getting those papers to the recycling facility in Brockton. The problem was the commitment from Dad and his car.

In the summer of 1964, at fourteen years of age, I went to work on a vegetable farm in the neighboring towne of Whitman. While working on the farm, I learned that not only was good behavior rewarded, but when I worked over and above what was expected of me came greater rewards and more friendships with those I worked with.

Each day that first summer, I woke up early and went to the kitchen to make a jelly and marshmallow sandwich wrapped in wax paper and placed in a brown bag that I would carry to the farm while riding my bike to get there. But along the way, I would eat it, since that daily trip just made me hungry. The farm owner was a giving man; when we had our morning break, he would allow us to go into the farm stand and select what we wanted. He bought them for us. I liked the job so much, and those I was working with, I applied myself more to what I was doing, learning how to pick the vegetables correctly.

One morning, while in the bean field, one of the other kids I was working with showed me how to increase the string beans in a bushel basket. He told me that when the basket was three-quarters full, you should place your hands at the bottom of the bushel and lift them up. I jostle them as I pull my hands towards the top. This increased the air between those beans, making it look like the basket was full. Thus, it would increase the number of bushels I would produce to send to the farm stand. However, those who worked the receiving platform knew of the trick, and so did the driver of the truck, as when I placed my bushels of beans on the truck, the jolting of those baskets settled the beans.

When they reached the platform, they counted the bushels I picked. Then they saw each bushel was less than what it should have been. They took from one of my other baskets and topped off those underfilled. I earned less than what I sent up. Each correctly filled bushel earned me twenty-five cents.

When I went to the owner to collect my pay for the morning, I noticed I was short twenty-five cents. The owner told me I underfilled those I sent up, which they had taken from one of those bushels to correct the others. I was pranked. I learned that when I placed the bushels on the back of the truck, the ride from the field to the farm stand jostled the beans in the basket, showing not an entire bushel. After that, I tried to exceed the expectations given to me while I worked there. I would prove myself to the lead farm hand, who was just an older kid than I; I was given better fields to pick vegetables from, where I would earn more money. I was also rewarded with more responsibility.

One morning, the lead worker did not show up for work. My first responsibility was training several new kids on picking peas and filling a bushel for maximum earnings. And to prevent them from being pranked by the same kid who did it to me.

Just before the end of my first summer and approaching the start of school, I was brought in from the field and was taught how to mix cement and lay cement blocks for the new addition to the farm store. This extended my employment and earnings well into the fall.

Irrigation Pond Party Fun

At the end of the 1964 summer, we kids who worked the field gathered by the farm's irrigation pond for a party. The farm owner generously provided sodas and snacks from his stand for us to enjoy.

The pond had a steep entry, making it challenging to jump from the shore. We found a long piece of wood lying around. It was about 12 inches wide and 12 feet long and pretty rough. Since the top of the board was rough, we wore our sneakers when jumping from it. The owner said we could have it since he had no use for it. We extended this board over the middle of the pond. But we needed something to anchor the board while some jumped off it. Our initial idea was to have several kids sit on the back end of the board to hold it steady while others dived from the other end. That plan flopped; once the diver leaped, those seated at the back were lifted off the board, causing our diving board to fall into the pond.

We spotted a large boulder, thinking we could muscle it over, but it barely budged. Then, one of the older kids fetched a tractor from the barn, equipped with forks at the front. We shifted the boulder onto the board's end with our combined strength and the tractor. This setup allowed us to walk out and jump into the water, and the board stayed put. No one had to sit on the backend. This outing marked our summer's end.

Earning Money Off-Season

In the fall of 1964, I started to rake leaves, but that abruptly ended when my dad suggested I help clear our yard and the elderly neighbor leaves for free!

Then, I thought I could try to earn additional income by collecting the neighbor's old newspapers again. I had no problem getting newspapers, but getting my dad to commit to helping me was challenging. He would be called in to work whenever a printing press went down. He was an electrician at the plant. Getting another adult to load their car to help was my next idea. My friend and neighbor, Richard, called his father to help. So it was Richard, me, his dad, and their 1965 Rambler wagon with the recycling business. This partnership lasted just that one winter until I returned to work on the farm in the Spring of 1965. I would also offer my services of shoveling driveways and sidewalks. I charged fifty cents an hour. I earned a whopping seven dollars for two days of work. Then, the competition for shoveling increased as my neighbor had purchased a snow plow to add to his jeep. My neighbors prefer plowing over a shoveler.

Farm Work Promotion

In the spring of 1965, I was asked to help with the planting and returned to being a farm field hand.

This one weekend, I received instructions on operating a tractor soon after returning to work. Mr. Clayton, the farm owner, was generous in allowing us youngsters to drive farm vehicles. I learned to drive the tractor and the plow implements that pulled behind it. Then I was taught to drive this old black 1949 Dodge pick-up that transported us, kids to sections of the field where we had to pick vegetables.

I thought this truck was the coolest thing I had ever learned to drive. It was a standard with a four-speed floor shift. Those who rode with me to the fields initially found it rough. But soon, I learned how to make a smoother transition in shifting and popping the clutch. Again, another lesson on driving that truck: don't pop a clutch when bringing those bushels of vegetables up to the farm stand. It was only once I did that as I had to pick up all the vegetables tipped over from all those bushels I was carrying.

However, my main task soon became wielding a hoe and diligently weeding the rows of young plants. Distinguishing between weeds and crops was a skill I had to acquire, as everything appeared to be a weed to me initially.

One late August morning, while picking peas, the head farm hand approached me and instructed me to see Mr.Clayton. Unsure of the reason for the summons, I hoped it wasn't bad news. Mr. Clayton, a gentle giant with an imposing presence, beckoned me closer. He commended my work ethic, punctuality, and willingness to assist others even when there was no direct benefit to me. Surprisingly, he promoted me from the field to a stockboy, assigning me to work inside the vegetable stand.

Working with those in the store brought me immense satisfaction. It caught the owner's attention, increasing my pay to sixty-five cents an hour. My primary work days were weekends, occasionally supplemented by a few weekdays. Weekends were bustling, with almost every young lad employed at the farm stand present.

I remained on the farm and worked in the farm stand until the end of autumn, when the last vegetables were harvested, marking the time to plow the fields for winter.

Working at D'Amatos

In January of 1966, I would be old enough for work, signaling the moment to earn a consistent income. I returned to D'Amatos, where I was caught stealing snacks, and submitted a job application. D'Amatos had an excellent reputation for hiring and a pleasing workplace.

I made my way to the store's small office in the back and asked for an application. Without looking up, Paul handed me the application and a pencil. While filling out my application, I kept my face down, fearing that Paul might look up and recognize me.

I completed the application and handed it back to him. He barely glanced at me; he jotted down a note on my application and asked me when I could start. Either he didn't recognize me, or he was giving me a second chance. Either way, he hired me on the spot. I started work the day after my sixteenth birthday and was paid one dollar twenty-five cents an hour working as a bag boy and stocker.

I needed that job as I was old enough to get my driver's license. And I needed to pay for my driver's education. It was a stipulation by my father as he would get a discount on the car insurance with my driver's ed. Also, it was Junior Prom year, and the girl I was dating, Amy, was a junior, and her prom was coming up. I needed to rent a tux and have money for the after-prom dinner. This would be the last and only Junior Prom or Senior Prom I would attend. It was Amy's and my last date; she wanted the summer of 1966 to date others as she started her senior year.

I had been employed at D'Amatos for nine months when she entered my world. Our initial encounter occurred in November of 1966 at the soda fountain of D'Amatos. People cross paths for various reasons that bring positivity; others do not. Some fleetingly pass through our lives, while others permanently etch themselves into our memories. She fell into the latter category.

Her arrival coincided with my tentative steps into adolescence. We both wandered through high school corridors, oblivious to the complexities of love's growth. Amid the teenage microcosm, the depth of emotions often took a backseat to the allure of casual dating and social interactions.

While stocking women's hygiene products one night, I noticed her presence at the soda fountain. Balancing my stocking duties with subtle glances in her direction, I hoped to remain unnoticed. I ran from restocking to bagging groceries, attempting to discreetly observe her. However, this new girl working at the soda fountain caught me staring at her, and in response, she smiled. I swiftly averted my gaze, presuming she hadn't noticed my staring. Nevertheless, she had, and her smile wasn't hidden from my perception.

Her charm was undeniable- the way she carried herself, the delicate curve of her slender neck, and the allure in her pretty brown eyes, nose, and lips made an irresistible invitation for a kiss. Her captivating gaze, framed by long, luscious eyelashes, held a deep, enchanting brown hue. Paired with her elegantly shaped lips, her smile was a silent masterpiece, subtly drawing me in. Yet, despite this magnetic pull, a sense of apprehension kept me from approaching her.

The Girl from a Neighboring Towne

The girl from the neighboring towne, the one who ignited a spark in my heart like no other. At first, we were both imprisoned by our shyness, trapped in a dance of stolen glances and averted eyes. Maybe it was mostly me, my heart pounding wildly every time her gaze found mine, causing me to hastily turn away as if my affections were contraband.

I was just your average high school boy. I was all of 5 foot 5 inches with average looks; not too bad a looking kid for the time, unlike the heartthrob Ricky Nelson, whose magnetic eyes drew in legions of teenage admirers. I was far from that league.

A member of the high school band and considered a *'band geek'* by some. I wore my passion on my sleeve. In contrast, she seemed to exude an aura of someone who only had eyes for football players to which I am worlds apart.

On my days off, I would make the pilgrimage to the store just to sit at the soda fountain and watch her and be near her presence. Pretending to be engrossed in some excuse while my real intention was just to catch glimpses of her. Those big beautiful brown eyes of hers were enchanting windows into her soul, to which my heart aches to look into.

Slowly, our orbits would align. Fate conspired to bring us together during shifts, or Paul, but our paths crossed more frequently. Working the same days and hours. I was almost afraid to believe in this newfound proximity as if it were too good to be true.

While this one night, when I was stocking products on the floor by the fountain, my thoughts and eyes were on her. I watched her glide from one end of the fountain to the other while very little was stocked on the shelves those nights. Then, as she left the fountain, went to the office, and checked out for the evening. I raced from placing the product on the shelve to the front register. I just made it before she came from around the corner of the fountain. She would pass by me, and as she did, she would say good night to me and those around me. Then she walked out to a car waiting for her in the front parking lot.

This one evening, I overlooked Paul in the area where I should have been stocking products, not watching this new girl. Fate's whims can be mischievous. Just as I was gearing up to make my move, I heard this voice booming from behind: Paul, a specter from the shadows, called me out as his words laced with jest and a knowing smirk. *'Are you working tonight, Crothers, or just staring at that girl?'* I answered him, *'Yes sir, making sure the new girl made it to her car.'* Then, turning and seeing Paul watching me, I saw his smirk and him saying to me, *'Looks like she made it out without your help, Crothers; now, how about you finishing your job so I can close up?'* A hasty retreat out the door beside Sharon, one of the cashiers, as she, too, was waiting on the stoop for her ride. Sharon had noticed me watching the new girl leave and asked why I didn't talk to her. I did not answer her but continued to watch the car that took her away. Then, turning to Sharon, I said, *'I sure would like to date her.'* Just as I said that, Sharon's ride arrived. She turned to me and told me I should just go ahead and ask her out. As Sharon left, I started walking to my car in the back parking lot where the employees parked. At least I know what towne she may live in the way the vehicle had headed.

Days passed, nerves fluttering like captive birds within me. The fear of rejection gripped my every step, but my desire to bridge the gap between us grew stronger. As the days melded into weeks, opportunity finally knocked a chance to drive her home.

I arrived early for work, hoping to see and talk to her. I wondered if I had enough courage even to speak to her. She was already at the fountain, so I took a seat away from all the other customers. There she was, making a fountain drink for a customer. Now she is walking towards me. A lump in my throat grew with each step she took toward me.

She was the most beautiful girl in all the high schools around. I can see her big brown eyes and long eyelashes; she smiles at me as she approaches. Most of all, she had the cutest little nose with those perfect lips. When she reached where I was sitting, she asked what I wanted; I could barely get the words out without tripping over them. *'A Coke, please.'* She turned and walked away, and I would watch her and every step she took going back to make my drink from the fountain.

She brought me my Coke; I stood up as she approached and noticed I was taller than her! Not much, maybe an inch or two. We had it all, just like two lovers. She placed my soft drink on the counter before me, and I picked it up and walked to the office to sign in.

I told her I would return for my break as I walked away. I signed in for work, then spent my entire evening walking from the front register via the snack bar to any part of the store just to see her. Even when I had to run to the back stockroom, I would pass the snack bar.

I knew I wanted to ask her out and stop this floundering around just passing by her. I just didn't have the nerve. I feared rejection from her.

Now in her third week working at D'Amatos, I decided I needed to ask her if I could drive her home after work. As I was coming to work this one day, I practiced how I would ask her if I could drive her home from work tonight. And it sounded pretty good as I heard it in my head. But then everything in my head sounded good! As I approached the store, my heart started to race, and my body began to shake. I entered the store and walked to the fountain when I heard her say, *'Hi, how are you today?'* I said I was okay and sat at the fountain farthest from her.

With my mind racing with all the possible rejections she could return with, I was ready to ask her my question. Then I heard her ask me if I wanted anything from the fountain. I said, *'Yes, I would like to know if I could drive you home after work.'* How stupid that sounded now that I asked her. I could feel my face turning red. I was unsure why, but I was nervous and excited to hear how she would answer my response. After waiting a long time for her to return to where I was seated with an answer, she returned with a Coke in her hand, and looking at me, she said, *'You have beautiful blue eyes. Did you know that?'* After which, she followed up with her answer to my question about driving her home, and the answer was *no*! Then she handed me my Coke and walked away.

I often wished that I was hired to work the fountain. But the store hired girls to work the fountain and to be the cashier. Leaving the boys to do stock and bagging. But what fun it would have been to work on the grill and fountain.

Now that she had said no to driving her home, my life seemed over. I looked dumbfounded as I stood staring at her. She looked at me with those big beautiful eyes, and my mouth dropped open at her response! I thought for sure she was going to say yes!

Was her saying no her way of leading me on? Or is she toying with my emotions, maybe playing hard to get? She just walked away, and as she did, she stopped, looked over her shoulder, and then said to me, *'Come back on your break.'* I got up from the fountain and walked to the office; leaving my soda behind, I signed in for work. Anticipation sings through my veins on what awaits me on my break.

This evening I was the second bag boy working with Sharon on the back register and stocking shelves. I also had a fifteen-minute break tonight.

As I worked the shift, I wondered what she might say and her answer would be.

Later, I returned to the fountain for my break. She noticed me walking toward her and pointed to where she wanted me to sit. She was smiling, and that made me nervous but encouraged. With a coke in her hand, I focused on her beautiful eyes as she walked towards me. Standing in front of me now, she begins. *'I said no when you asked if you could take me home tonight because I already have a ride and cannot change it.'* she continued, *'I need a ride to work Saturday morning.'* She asked if I could pick her up and bring her to work. I said yes! Then she handed me her address and phone number on the napkin she had in her hand. After my break, the back register bell rang, indicating Sharon needed a bagboy. When I arrived, Sharon asked me why I screamed out *yes*. I told her I was picking up the new girl on Saturday and bringing her to work. *'Good for you,'* Sharon said, ringing the customer with the speed for which Sharon was known. I went to work bagging the order and struggling to keep up with the groceries she was sending down the conveyor belt to where I was bagging them.

After my break, the fountain was shut down for the evening. The fountain would close thirty minutes before the store, allowing those working it to clean the grill, wash the glasses and dishes, and sweep behind and in front of the counter area.

Front registers would close first, and any customers in the store would check out using the back register. Since we had more than the usual number of late shoppers this evening, the front registers stayed open to get them cashed out. She left using the front doors tonight since the registers were still open. I moved from Sharon's back register to the front registers to watch her leave and to see who was picking her up. As she passed, she said, *'Don't forget to pick me up now.'*

Being Friday night, it was rare for me not to go out. Those of my friends who did not work had made other plans earlier. Either a date or going to places where you would meet girls to make dates. But that night, I had nothing to do and no date. I just drove home and went to bed early. It is so unusual for a teenage boy with a driver's license.

Saturday morning came, and I got up and used my dad's electric shaver to shave that morning, whisking off whatever I thought was growing on my face. Then, splashing on enough English Leather to hide any sweat that may occur, I walked past my mother, and she noticed the smell, but said nothing.

In December, the band had no more football games to attend. We, the band, had gone into winter concert season, so I could work more hours at the store on Saturdays.

As I was all ready for work, I sat in the kitchen when my mother came in to make her coffee. She asked me why all the fuss with myself today, and I replied just work, she left the kitchen, headed back to her room, and woke dad.

This particular morning felt like it was moving slowly. When I finally left the house, I had to make a few diversions to her home. My timing was off, as I thought it would have taken longer than it did to find her house. First, I drove past her street several times; the first was to ensure I was correct in the location of her home and see it. I looked at my watch as I passed her house, only seven minutes later than when I left home. I was going to be at her house on time. I continued to drive around in circles around her street until it was time to pick her up.

I arrived at her house promptly at 8:30 a.m. The store opened at 9:00 a.m., giving us enough time. She was on her porch, ready as I pulled up to the curb on her street. I got out and raced toward the passenger side door. As she had already started walking toward the car.

Beautiful Girl in Car

As she approached, my heart raced. She was a vision, gliding toward me in that plaid skirt that swayed with each step, a white blouse accentuating her delicate features. Those knee-high socks, perfectly complementing the ensemble, added a touch of innocence that made her irresistible. She exuded a charm uniquely hers in those penny loafers, effortlessly captivating my teenage gaze. Her work smock in hand seemed like an afterthought, overshadowed by her enchanting presence. When she stopped in front of my car, time seemed to pause, allowing me to soak in every detail of her ethereal beauty.

My pride and joy, the 1957 Buick Special, stood there, a gift from my parents that symbolized freedom and adventure. Anticipation surged as I rushed to open her door, wanting to make her entrance into the car as graceful as she was. The way she thanked me, her elegance evident even in the simple gesture, made my heart flutter. She moved gracefully, effortlessly slipping into the car despite the constraints of her skirt. Today, adorned in her skirt, was a sight to behold. I watched her slowly glide across the bench seat; I couldn't help but feel captivated by her every movement.

But fate played its hand, and in my attempt to hurry back to the driver's side, I stumbled and fell embarrassingly before her. The clumsiness left me red-faced, and though I assured her I was fine, the pain in my skinned knee lingered. Concealing the injury beneath dark pants, I spent the day hiding the discomfort, grateful that the bloodstain appeared more like a spill. At work, I tried to wash away the evidence in the restroom, remaining hidden until I deemed the pants presentable enough to face the world.

As we drove away from her house, I wanted to ask her if she had a boyfriend and why he was not taking her to work. We asked each other questions, and I feared her answers. I hoped her response to one of my questions would be that she had no boyfriend. She turned, looked at me, and said, *'What makes you think I have a boyfriend?'* My stomach was churning, so nervous from asking that question; she answered. So, I repeated her question, *'Why did I ask you that?'* I said, *'Because you're so pretty, I would have thought you would have a boyfriend, and I didn't want to be used for a confrontation with him as it was not on my list of things I like!'* I continued, *'The other night, you got into a car with another guy when you left work.'* The pain from my skinned knee was nothing like I thought I would feel if she said she had a boyfriend. She smiled back at me. Then while laughing, she told me that her brother had picked her up that evening. She asked me if I was seeing anyone, and I said, *'No.'* She told me that she had been seeing someone, but they had broken up. We continued our conversation, and I found myself never at a loss for words with her from then on.

We arrived at work long before we had to and sat and talked in the car when she asked me how late I would be working. I told her until 5:00 p.m.. She said that she had to work till 5:00 p.m. as well and asked if I could give her a ride home after work. I have now answered the question, *'Do you like me?'* I said, *'Yes'* to her question and that I would take her home after work.

We walked into work, signed in, and went our respective ways. I looked at today's schedule and who I would be working with. Today, I had the back register with a classmate's mother, Mrs. Rodgers, and next week's schedule Paul had posted, would be working with Sharon.

Mrs. Rodgers expected nothing but the best from her bag boys and to keep up with her as she rang her customers up. She also expected her bag boys to pack her customers' groceries correctly and lightly and never put bread and eggs at the bottom.

When I started learning to pack bags, I overpacked the first bag I packed on my own, placing many cans with the customer's bread and eggs on the bottom. That customer returned with crushed bread and broken eggs. Since this was a small town, most knew the supermarket's owners. And they did not hesitate to call if there was a problem with their packed groceries!

This one time, shortly after I started to work there, this woman must have upset Paul with her complaint as Paul came to find me. I still think I'm on a shoestring with him if he ever remembers I was the one he tossed out for stealing. While bagging at the register, he approached me and directed me to follow him. As I did, I wondered what he had in store for me: a new assignment? Nope! He told me of the call he had received from a customer about the way I bagged her groceries. Then Paul made me work with one of the older boys who had been there longer and would teach me how to bag groceries properly. This was when I met my two new friends, both seniors at South Shore Vocational Technical High School. Who knew there was a right way to bag??

It took a long time before I was allowed to bag for Mrs. Rodgers after that incident! But I became very good at bagging, which landed me better tips!

Getting To Know Each Other

Almost every evening, I made it a routine to accompany the new girl out after our shift at the store. Serendipitously, our boss, Paul, scheduled us for the same hours and days, allowing our paths to intertwine too frequently. On occasions when our schedules diverged, I willingly journeyed to her school, ensuring she got to work and later returned to escort her home. Each instance reinforced our bond, nurturing a connection that deepens every day.

One serene evening, as dusk painted the sky in soft hues of lavender and indigo, we nestled in the quiet embrace of her neighborhood. The gentle breeze carried the distant murmur of windows opened in houses- hints of T.V. shows' dialogue muffled yet distinct. The stars, radiant in their celestial dance, adorned the velvet canvas above, casting a shimmering glow that seemed to amplify the tranquility of the night.

Turning towards me, her eyes held a playful sparkle as if inviting secrets to be shared under the canopy of the night sky. Let's delve beyond the confines of work, she suggested with a smile, her voice carrying the warmth of a shared moment. I want to discover more about the layers that make you, you.

She started the conversation by mentioning her job as a lifeguard at the town pool last summer. But that job ended after labour day as school was back in session. She wanted to earn more money to purchase the clothes that she liked and made her look good. She needed a job while school was in session and found that job at D'Amatos. She applied to be a cashier where she could work with all the good-looking boys that would bag for her. But Paul only offered her the snack bar position he needed help in. She says that she wants to dive deeper into my world. *'So, spill the beans,'* she teased, *'what's your story?'*

I chuckled and told her I had worked at Clayton Farms on Plymouth Street before I began working at D'Amatos. *'Wait, Clayton Farms?* she says. *'I know that place; my mother and I would go there to get our vegetables as they were better than the local markets' produce. I thought that is why you looked familiar to me.'* I told her I would have remembered you had I seen you there.

Not realizing she was the smart one in this soon-to-be relationship, she was cleverly asking questions about my past. Connecting the dots with each query.

Among our shared interests, she surprised me by telling me how she enjoys candlepin bowling. A type of bowling that uses smaller balls and pins that are thinner and taller than ten-pin bowling. It didn't surprise me because, in candlepin, you have to use more finesse than sheer power, as in ten-pin bowling. And she was nothing short of finesse. Another discovery in our tapestry of mutual passions.

As we continued spending time together, she shared her love for roller skating at our local rink, particularly when it was not so crowded. She liked how, when she would watch, other couples glided and swayed to the music in each other's embrace and wished she could also experience that type of skating. Moreover, she said she would enjoy ice skating at Hobart Pond, especially after the city had installed a pole light for evening skating, creating a delightful setting. As for movies, we both favored drive-in theaters over indoor ones.

And she shared just how much she loved the beach, not so much for swimming, but for long walks along the shore. Sharing special moments with ourselves, searching for answers to those mindless questions in our heads. *'God, will I ever find love?'* and knowing when we did find love, we could share those silent moments without talking. That's when we both knew we were with the right person. She knew, but I didn't realize that she knew.

On one of our drives to her house after work, she confessed about her kissing prowess. Instead of her getting out of the car and going into the house, we parked outside her home, using those few minutes to practice before the flickering of the front porch light signaling the passage of time, a testament to the enchantment of our shared moment.

With us in an intimate embrace, her lips, as soft as silk, melded perfectly against mine as I held her close. She whispered softly into my ear that her kissing prowess was not what boys liked. *'They always seemed to want more from my kisses,'* she said, *'I just was not ready to give more to them.'*

Then, the signal of the porch light came, the flickering of the light. She better get inside and now! I knew I best get her onto the porch if I wanted to go out with her again. We exited the car and walked hand in hand up the steps to the porch. A single low-wattage light lit the porch. Those porch lights only remained on when someone was out from the family. Then, they would turn off the light to save on the electricity. We stood before the door, holding each other's hands and talking. We weren't ready to part ways with each other. I placed my arms around her and pulled her close; we continued to speak, with kisses in between. This continued until her father hollered out to us again for her to come inside. She opened the main door to the house and said, *'Daddy, I'll be right in.'* She had such command over her father. He replied, *'Hurry up, that light is costing me money just to have you and your boyfriend playing kissy face!'*

We stood in the doorway for another five minutes when she pulled me close to her, giving me my final goodnight kiss. I believe she may have given me the kiss all the other boys had wanted. The kiss that lasted forever. Then we said goodnight.

Our First Date
Blue Love Memories

Our first date unfurled like a vibrant canvas, painted with the spirited presence of my friend Bob and his effervescent partner, Janice. The evening beckoned us to a local theater in Brockton. The silver screen shimmered in this place, promising to transport us into otherworldly realms. Yet, fate had a different script written for us that night. Nestled at the back of the theater, in seats that cradled us clandestinely, we were enraptured not by the cinematic magic but by an enchanting dance of stolen kisses and shared whispers.

The allure of the movie dimmed beneath the radiant chemistry igniting between us. Our world revolved within that secluded enclave, oblivious to the on-screen spectacle. As the credits rolled, our journey continued, propelled by the magnetic pull of Papa Ginos, a local pizza parlor exuding an irresistible charm that beckoned us forth.

It wasn't merely a place for pizzas; it was a haven brimming with character, a stone's throw away from the theater, where the aroma of freshly baked dough intertwined with the burgeoning connection, weaving a fragrant narrative of a night etched in the indelible ink of burgeoning romance.

As we left the movie theater and returned to the car, the night air was cold, and we ran briskly to the car. Settling into the car seats, the familiar comfort enveloped us as we turned on the radio. Then, in the coziness of the car, a new song was introduced, Love is Blue. It had a haunting melody that lodged into my memory as a song that would bring back the night of our first date.

Yet, amidst the lingering echoes of the tune, the enticing smells from Papa Gino beckoned. The aroma of the freshly baked pizza teased our senses, influencing our decision to venture over to the restaurant our evening meal, pizza.

Our arrival at Papa Ginos was without fanfare; this place was such fun. Imagine an old-time ragtime-sounding piano and its melodies dancing through the air every Friday and Saturday night, adding nostalgia to the atmosphere.

We settled around long communal tables, sharing the space with fellow pizza enthusiasts. Bob might not have been a singing virtuoso. Still, he was the conductor of our merry melody group's laughter and joy. His exuberance was infectious, and when he belted out tunes, any thoughts of pitch perfection melted away.

Bob was a character straight out of a T.V. show, reminiscent of Bill Gray's character on 'Father Knows Best.' The uncanny similarities extended to his cars, mirroring those driven by Billy Gray on screen. It was like encountering a real-life doppelganger. At Papa Gino's, our voices intertwined, each note celebrating life itself. It didn't matter if we hit all the right notes; what counted was the shared euphoria and bond that we were building.

The four of us wove an evening tapestry of pure delight. Amidst laughter and the savory aroma of pizza, Bob, a former D'Amatos employee, probed my date about our story's origin. With a blush from that face of an angel and a shy smile, she recounted the tale of our first meeting. She said, 'A diligent shelf stocker, he was stationed across from the soda fountain restocking an array of feminine products.' With that, I said, 'Even now, the names of those products have the power to color my cheeks.'

Time seemed to stretch as we basked in each other's company, the world outside fading into insignificance. Her beauty and smile lit up my whole world wherever we went. And then we left and headed back to our homes. Bob dropped us off, where we met him and Janice, and I drove her home from our date.

Winter Drive-In Romance

Winter chill couldn't extinguish our adventurous spirit. Even in those frosty months, a few drivers braved the weather. As we pulled into the drive-in theater, the attendants kindly handed us an L.P. heater to help keep us warm while watching the movie.

We wrapped ourselves in blankets and huddled close. We lit the propane heater with a sense of excitement. However, its pungent aroma left much to be desired, so we discreetly moved it outside the car. Our quest for warmth was only beginning, but my natural desire was to watch her.

With the heater banished, we sought warmth in each other's arms. Our breath mingled in the frosty air as we shared stories, dreams, and stolen kisses. Occasionally, intricate patterns of frost painted themselves on the windshield, momentarily obscuring our view of the movie. Yet truth be told, we hardly mind. The thrill of staying cozy together wrapped up in our world, eclipsed any storyline on the screen.

The night marked more than just a date; it was the start of an epic journey. An adventure sewn together with laughter, warmth, and the magic of shared moments. Our love story was born that night, a symphony of joy and the prelude to a love that would endure beyond the seasons.

When we Fell in Love
A New Chapter in Life

In the tapestry of my youth, woven with moments both fleeting and enduring, there exists a singular thread that glistens with the sparkle of Christmas Lights and the rhythm of laughter: Edaville Railroad. It wasn't merely a park; rather, it stood as a sanctuary of enchantment, cradled amidst the towering fragrant pine trees and embraced by the wintry charm of the holiday season. My fondest memories coalesced around that enchanting visit orchestrated by the parents of my dearest friend. It was a pilgrimage to a wonderland where the air was infused with the fragrance of evergreens and the sounds of joy from children's laughter that echoed through the frosty air.

I remember the thrill of that visit, a treasure chest of delights waiting to be unlocked. It wasn't merely a place but a childhood dream, a realm where the ordinary would be transformed into the extraordinary. Each glittering light, fallen snowflakes, and, of course, the whimsical train ride etched into the fabric of my being, imprinting an ineradicable mark on my heart.

For years after that first visit, Edaville Railroad would linger as a cherished memory, a radiant symbol I yearned to share with someone special someday. Yet fate interceded, weaving circumstances intertwined tightly with the constraints of youth, leaving me distanced from that wintry wonderland until the day came when the reins of freedom were finally handed to me in the form of car keys.

Our Love Story Begins

Our love story unfolds beneath the twinkling lights of Edaville Railroad, where time seemed to slow down, and magic danced in the air. It was a winter tale that began when I was still young and the world was a canvas of wonder waiting to be painted with the colors of love.

Edaville Railroad is a place born from the dreams of a visionary named E.D. Atwood. Held within its tracks a symphony of history and enchantment, a story woven with locomotives and passenger cars carried by the rhythmic chug of a steam train through the heart of cranberry bogs. Nestled in South Carver, this place held the very essence of a love story.

In the winter of 1966, we embarked on a journey that would forever intertwine our hearts. A canvas brushed with starlight colors of romance. The air was crisp, infused with the scent of evergreens, popcorn, and the warmth of hot apple cider.

She was wrapped in an ensemble that teased warmth, and a hint of tantalizing charm turned heads effortlessly. Her attire was a delightful fusion of elegance and allure, with a plaid skirt that hugged her curves and a cozy sweater that hinted at the softness underneath. Her knee-high socks accentuated the length of her legs, teasingly drawing attention to every step she took, exuding a timeless grace.

To brave the winter chill, she draped herself in a mid-length coat that cascaded gracefully down to her knees, tantalizingly accentuating her silhouette. A scarf hugged her neck, enhancing her grace in every movement. Knowing their effect on me, her penchant for skirts showcased her stunning legs, a feature I always admired.

The evening air painted a gentle, rosy hue on her cheeks, heightening the natural radiance that perpetually emanated from her. Her choice of skirts hinted at our playful adventures, sparking a delightful change once she returned home.

Walking hand in hand beneath the colorful lights that adorned our path, we felt the universe conspiring to make this night unforgettable.

It is where I fell in love with every move of her. Every glance into her enchanting brown eyes felt like diving into a world of warmth and tenderness, each sparkle in her smile a constellation of joy. The memories of our date at Edaville lingered as the most magical moments etched in my mind. In this place, the symphony of love composed itself, where I discovered the enchantress, that is her. There, the seeds of an extraordinary love story were sown, blossoming into the grandest of passions.

We purchased our train excursion tickets, then walked around the park and looked at all the decorations while the train circled the cranberry bog with its first load of riders. Then we walked through the museum quickly towards the train station. We talked amongst ourselves about where we wanted to ride on the train. Did we want to ride in the open or enclosed train cars? We decided to sit in the train coach, where there were heaters, with prompting from our dates. Bob and I wanted the open-air train cars but gave way to what the girls wanted.

Standing on the station platform, we watched the train come down the tracks, plumes of steam billowing from the engine. I wanted her to be close, so I placed my arms around her waist and pulled her near me. I looked into her eyes and saw the sparkle of delight. And her smile that she so often wore lured me in to kiss her. That brought joy to me. She reached for my hand and, taking it, moved it into her coat pocket.

'Are your hands cold?' she asked.

'A little,' I replied.

She then placed her head on my shoulder. I knew at that moment, it was her, who should be in my life.

As we continued to stand on the platform, the train slowed down as it passed us. Standing close to the platform's edge, the steam from the air brakes came out and filled the air around us.

The engine bell began to clang out loudly as it passed. Then the engineer gave several toots from its engine whistle, a signal which we had to remove our hands from her warm jacket to cover our ears.

She whispered that she preferred to be inside during this ride and thanked me for understanding. It was because she was wearing a skirt on our date. We stood on the platform next to the stairs of the enclosed car coach, waited until those on the ride were off, and hurriedly climbed aboard.

The steam train, our chariot of destiny, awaited to carry us on a journey around the cranberry bogs. The locomotive whispered promises of adventure as it steamed and purred, a testament to the magic that awaited. As we boarded the train, the world seemed to fade away, leaving only us in a cocoon of woven dreams. I could not live without her and wanted to marry her.

We found two seats near the entrance of the coach, so we moved fast to sit in those seats near the front. As she slid onto the seat and sat beside the large glass window, I sat beside her. Bob and Janice took the seats in front of us and faced us.

Not long after we were seated, my arm was around her shoulder, bringing her tight against me. The train car was dimly lit, with just enough light cast for me to see her reflection in the window. As we sat there, I noticed that Jack Frost had started working on the window from her breath. *'Are you creating that ice drawing?'* I asked. She turned with her sheepish smile and said, *'Maybe.'* I found myself entranced, observing her silhouette in the window's reflection, pondering the thoughts that occupied her mind. Suddenly, she turned towards me, planting a gentle kiss on my cheek before resuming her gaze out into the enveloping darkness beyond. I kept watching her through the reflection in the window. Wondering what her thoughts were. She turned toward me and kissed me on my cheek, then went back, looking out the window and gazing into the darkness.

As I gently lowered the collar of her jacket, I leaned in, my lips finding their way to her long, slender neck. A shiver coursed through her, a delicate tremor I might have provoked with the gentlest of touches. She gracefully turned, granting me access to her lips, and our kiss deepened.

We shared an ease in our affection, never hesitating to exchange kisses. Yet, amidst our intimacy, this uncanny sensation surfaced in my mind of a possibility that we might have crossed paths in another time and another era, where our souls entwined in a timeless chapter in our lives; eternal soul connection.

As we sat in our seats, the train began its embarkment on whisking us on tonight's magical journey. With each movement, a force is transmitted, a jerking of each car, and those seated in each car are pushed forward and then pulled back into their seat. It's like a back-and-forth rocking motion. All of this happens while we hear those classic toots from the train whistle. It's akin to a choreographed dance, where we are seamlessly drawn into the train's graceful momentum, feeling the sheer power as it glides away from the station.

We could hear the engine chug as we pulled out of the station, now gathering speed; as it did, larger amounts of steam came from its tall stack and passed by our window.

With the shrill of its whistle warning people as we approached the crossing. We slowly chugged by; those standing at the gate would wave to those of us on the train. We would wave back to them as we rode by. In the background, laughter was heard from the smaller children riding with us in our coach.

Hearing the children's laughter and cries of joy riding the rails of this Christmas adventure in tonight's chariot, my thoughts turned to us having our children someday and riding this train with them and maybe even our grandchildren. Bringing our family back during our golden wedding anniversary would be fantastic, to show them where we fell in love.

Moving along faster, we circled the cranberry bog, where colorful lights adorned the bogs and levee. As we circled the bog, the weather started to change. Snowflakes began to fall, delicate and gentle, as if nature painted a portrait of our love.

As we passed one of the frozen bogs, a dreamscape revealed. The ice shimmered beneath the glow of the surrounding lights, a canvas upon which the essence of winter danced. Skaters, like poetry in motion, swirled and twirled with captivating grace. As we traced the perimeter in our Christmas train, this evening was truly an enchanting spectacle.

The falling snow added a new prism to the magical setting, casting everything in a soft, romantic veil. It was as though nature herself conspired to enhance the beauty of this moment, painting an exquisite portrait of our love against the wintry backdrop.

Still, her beauty that night was ethereal, a reflection of the winter grace. Her eyes held the promise of a thousand stories, and her smile was a constellation of stars that lit up my heart. Still gazing out her window, she watched the falling snow intensely.

As I sat, watching her reflection in the window, I wondered what her thoughts were. Were they of us? And then she turned toward me, smiling, kissing me on my cheek, then declaring,

> 'You know I can see you looking at me in the window.'

I said nothing but smiled back at her, enjoying the moment we sat together as we circled the bog and watched those colored lights go by.

Our journey through the cranberry bog and seeing its colored lights became enchanted; the romance of riding this old steam train made for a beautiful, lasting memory of this evening.

Along the way, I would pull her close as the train's wheels started their melodious dance, each clickety-clack resonating with the rhythm of my heartbeat.

As the train continued its way through the bogs, our journey mirrored our hearts' path. Her presence beside me felt like a gift from the universe, and with each passing moment, my love for her grew even more robust.

Her soft breath lingered, tracing delicate frost patterns on the windowpane, a tangible echo of the beautiful vulnerability that comes with the dance of falling in love.

In the dimly lit train car, we shared stolen moments of tenderness. Her slender and smooth neck, a canvass of grace, invited my kisses, and her lips, soft as the newly fallen snowflakes outside, whispered promises of forever.

The train's whistle sang tales of adventure as our world outside blurred into a kaleidoscope of color and lights. With threads of tapestry woven, children's laughter and golden anniversaries celebrate the love we had found in this place.

Reality began to tug at the edges of our enchanted evening as the train neared the station. But time was no match for the love between us. We held onto each other, savoring the final moments of our journey, not wanting the night or the train ride to end.

The train station was now coming into view as we approached the end of the ride. Beginning to slow down, its engine's whistle signals our arrival as we near the station.

Families hurriedly gathered their belongings inside our car, a symphony of motion to prepare to embrace the cold again. But we had remained seated. We watched parents holding their children and gathering their belongings. Children in oversized winter coats, which all mothers thought they would grow into. And fathers now putting on those red and black checkered hats on their sons and making sure the ear flaps were over their child's ears as their mothers beckoned out to them.

They all looked like Elmer Fudd with those hats, as if they were going hunting. Chuckling and turning to her, I tell her how I remembered my mother placing that hat on my head and sending me out to play in the snow. And then I quietly asked, *'Our boys will not look like that, will they?'*

She was too beautiful to produce Elmer Fudds! And those knit caps grandma made for the girls last Christmas are now being worn and tied under their chin. Wait till they see the pictures of themselves years from now. With them all bundled up they depart the train and head out into the cold.

We remained seated for several minutes, watching the people pass. Occasionally, I could see a smile on her face as the children looked at her as they walked by. Maybe they were thinking the same thing I was: how pretty she is. Then she would turn to me and comment on how cute the kids looked, all dressed in winter coats. Some had scarves wrapped entirely around their face, leaving only enough openings to see their eyes. Still, their eyes would continue looking at her as they passed by.

Quickly being shuffled, the kids hurried to the train's exit and out to their next adventure. After the last family moved past us, we got up from our seats, and I reached for her hand and held on to it so as not to lose each other in the crowd.

We walked in the night's cold air for several minutes before going to the museum to warm up. There, we purchased hot cocoa. It kept our hands warm. I turned and looked at her and said we could bring our kids here for the train ride someday. She just smiled at me as if to say that would be nice.

Once back at the car, Bob asked us where we wanted to go. *'How about we have some dinner,'* I said. We talked it over, and then we mentioned Cranberry House. This is a newer restaurant and was decorated in all cranberry colors. It's just a simple place to have burgers and ice cream. It was also a place where we could go and stay warm, sit, and talk for hours.

Bob suddenly turned down this dirt road as we drove from the parking lot. We sat there for several minutes as the cars behind us passed by. *'Which Cranberry House,'* Bob asked. *'How about the one in Hanover,'* someone called out. We all agreed to that. Bob backed the car out of the woods onto the road, and off we went.

D.W. Fields Park

Spring has now bloomed, painting the world in shades of green and floral fragrances of lilacs. This one Sunday in April was particularly warm, and we decided to picnic at the park in Brockton. I found an old blanket we could use to lay on the ground and tossed it in the car's back seat. Then I drove over to her house to pick her up. She was standing on the porch when I arrived, just a vision of loveliness. She had prepared a special lunch for us on this special day. I met her about halfway up the sidewalk. We stopped and kissed, and I took her basket and carried it to the car. I opened her car door and placed the basket on the back seat near the blanket. She slides into the front seat. Then, once I get in, we drive off and head out to D.W. Fields Park for our picnic.

The weather was warm, and the sun gently kissed our skin, making it the perfect day for an outdoor excursion. The park was a serene haven with a tranquil pond, making that spot cozy and perfect for our picnic. As I spread the blanket, we spied two swans gracefully swimming toward us. Grabbing a few pieces of bread we began tossing bits of it to those elegant creatures.

As we basked in the serenity of the afternoon, she turned to me and, with a twinkle in her eye and asked if we could go to the amusement park. Her enthusiasm was contagious, and she convinced me that an adventure to one of our local Amusement Parks would be the perfect place for us to end our day. I agreed with her; we packed up the remnants of our picnic, leaving only the fond memories of our idyllic waterside interlude, setting off for Nantasket Beach.

Lincoln Park

Lincoln Park is a nostalgic teen haven of amusement and joy, where laughter filled the air as visitors of all ages reveled in its offerings. Nestled in a compact space, the park boasted a charming dance hall reminiscent of bygone days and a bustling roller skating rink that hosted thrilling Friday night dance competitions. The pervasive scent of freshly popped popcorn wafted throughout the park, adding to its enchantment. At the same time, the rides dazzled in a kaleidoscope of colors.

Sunday, 1967, Labor Day weekend, we decided to spend our day at Lincoln Park. Where we worked closed on Sunday. The warmth of this September day enveloped us, accentuating Pam's sun-kissed legs that shone brightly as she decided to wear her shorts that day. Her hair danced in the breeze that emanated from the nearby ocean, and her eyes sparkled with an allure that never failed to captivate me.

Established in 1894 as a destination for working-class families to enjoy picnics amidst the surrounding pine groves, Lincoln Park had evolved over the years, introducing rides in 1920. To transform into a full-fledged amusement park.

FROM THE COLLECTION OF BOB CROTHERS- SEPTEMBER 1967

The park has a diverse array of rides. There was a dedicated section for younger children, but we were drawn to the more thrilling attractions.

The Comet roller coaster was a particular favorite. The thrill of the steep drop and the curves that we experienced made it all the more thrilling.

The Merry-Go-Round, in all its glory of colored horses, lions, tigers, and seats, allowed us to hold each other's hands. Even when the horses we rode rhythmically ascended and descended to the music.

The dodge-m-cars, or bumper cars, offered a delightful chance to collide playfully with loved ones or potentially make new acquaintances through friendly collisions. Amidst the plethora of midway games, I tried my luck, hoping to win a giant stuffed animal, but little did I know that the love we shared was a far more valuable prize than any plush toy I could win for her.

The Ferris wheel afforded panoramic views of the park, especially when it reached the top.

The tilt-a-whirl spun us around, pressing us closer to each other.

We stumbled upon a recording booth in the Penny Arcade. We contemplated creating a lasting memory by singing a song of a popular tune- a thoughtful keepsake to commemorate our day there.

My favorite ride was the Monster Ride funhouse; cloaked in darkness, I could hold her close and savor her kisses until the ride ended.

After indulging in several rides, we decided to take a break and walked over to the roller skating rink. As the more skillful skaters glide past us, we commented on their beauty and grace, making it look like they are effortlessly skating forward and backward. While many others passed by with their weaving gracefully, some holding onto each other while they circled the rink, and we marveled at their talent.

Returning to the ride section of the park, we observed the younger children's unbridled joy as they reveled in their rides, pointing and laughing as they spun by us. In those carefree moments, we shared our dreams of one day bringing our children to Lincoln Park, wondering if they would create beautiful memories here.

We indulged in a few more rides before we headed to the beach to continue our afternoon adventure together.

The Beach
The summer of 1967

As we drove to the beach, Pam's hair billowed in the breeze as we had the car windows down. As we cruised towards the beach, her hand danced in the slipstream, mimicking the rhythm of an airplane's elevator. Her smile radiated warmth and joy.

She moved closer as we continued to drive, turning sideways and draping her arm around my neck, her head nestled on my shoulder as she declared, *'This is an absolutely splendid day; I wish it could last forever.'*

The beach we visited is accessed by the Powder Point Bridge and Gurnet Road near what remained of the Civil War Fort Andrew and Fort Standish. The allure of the history mingled with the shore's natural beauty created a sense of wonder as we stepped onto the sandy expanse.

When we arrived, nature greeted us in all its diversity. The beach is a canvas painted with life and a vibrant variety of wildlife.

Shoes off and a sparkle in her eye, we raced each other to reach the base of the first dune. As we stopped at the bottom, the sea breeze lightly blew across our bodies, and we could smell the salt air. The small amount of seagrass that grew along the base of the dune would whisk against our calves, and gentle sea breezes encouraged us to move quickly away from it.

Paused to catch our breath, our anticipation building with each passing second. Side by side, we embarked on the ascent, the sand playfully slipping away beneath our feet, challenging our progress. Yet, we conquered the incline hand in hand, arriving victorious at the summit.

In the excitement, we slid down the dune with carefree abandonment. The cascade of sand marks our descent onto the shoreline. Our friendly competition of chasing after each other as we ran out to catch the tide making its way in and to us resume the goal of reaching the tide line and leaving our footsteps in the sand before the rolling waves could reclaim our footprints.

Her eyes seemed to hold the very essence of the sunlight, casting a warm, golden glow upon her. Anticipation in the air was palpable. We strolled along the sand, wrapped in each other's arms and her skin against mine. It felt so pure and soft to the touch, like the finest silk.

Our fingers entwined, we turned and gazed deeply into each other's eyes. We found an undeniable connection within the depth, a love that words could fail to capture.

Exchanging wordless glances that spoke volumes, we both understood the unspoken excitement that lay ahead. With her little evil laugh, she looked at me. Her gaze shifted towards the sprawling beach before us, and with a playful challenge, she declared, *'Race you down the tide line.'* A mischievous glint danced in her eyes as her laughter bubbled up like a shared secret. It was on from that point. That single phrase marked the beginning of our adventure.

Standing now at the water's edge, we could sense the ebb and flow of the tide, its rhythmic dance mirroring our emotions. The ocean's expanse stretched boundlessly before us, a sight that stirred a profound connection between us and the world around us. Our hands found each other, interwinding as we watched the waves in their eternal chase. With the unspoken agreement, we set off down the beach, our steps attuned with one another; the waters embrace a playful reminder of life's simple joys.

The tide ebbed and flowed, its gentle touch teasing our toes as it beckoned us toward the sea. Each wave that caressed our feet seemed to whisper secrets of the ocean's timeless wisdom and drew us closer to its embrace.

The sand is soft and cool beneath our feet, creating a sensation akin to a gentle massage. Laughter echoed as we engaged in a spirited game of tag with the encroaching tide. We were adolescents ensnared by the enchantment of first love, every splash of water and peal of laughter etching memories into our hearts. The coldness of the water was inconsequential compared to the warmth that radiated between us.

Minutes transformed into moments suspended in time, the shoreline an ever-shifting canvas for our shared experiences. Amid the splashes and jest, stolen glances grew bolder until our lips met in a fleeting kiss. A simple gesture shifted the dynamic, my arm encircling her waist, drawing her nearer. Her head rested gently on my shoulder. Her embrace is a testament to our connection. The day felt infinite as we conversed, a sentiment that only strengthened our relationship.

After walking a few hundred feet, we reached a spot on the beach where we decided to sit and just hold each other while watching the ocean tide come in for the evening.

The sun now setting on our backs, keeping us warm, as the ocean breeze grew chilly. We pushed our feet into the sand and wiggled our toes to bury them deeper and deeper into the soft, damped sand and to keep them warm.

Saying nearly not a word to one another, we just sat, continued staring out over the water, and watched people passing by. The closeness of what we had would never end as we held on to each other. It was as if our love coursed through one another's veins. During this time, my love for her grew even more potent.

As we continued to sit, we told each other how we wished we had more time to be together that day. We continued looking out over the horizon and at the endless water. I would caress her soft silky shoulders as the smell of the salt air surrounded us. She was what dreams were made of, and one I would hope for as my lifelong partner.

The ocean breeze became a little chillier as day became evening, and the sun descended, painting the sky with vibrant hues of orange and pink; we made our way to the beach's edge, where the dunes awaited. It was time to walk back to the car. With laughter and the thrill of the moment, we raced each other to the summit, our footsteps dancing amidst the seagrass. Its soft, swaying embrace whispered love to our hearts, a promise of an everlasting bond that would remain as constant as the sea and the sand.

When we arrived at the car, we put our shoes back on. The one thing you could not do was remove enough sand from between your toes to make wearing shoes comfortable. Lucky for Pam, she brought sandals on this date.

After a sun-kissed day at the beach, where laughter mingled with the ocean melody and the warmth of sand embraced us, we sought Howard Johnson for a twilight dinner. As we sat across each other in our booth, the sun setting even more on the western horizon front, painting colors upon the sky in hues that mirrored the joy in our hearts, fingers gently entwined, imprinting this moment into the tapestry of our cherished memories that spoke of our love.

Friendship Ring

On a chilly afternoon in October of 1967, I embarked on a journey that would forever etch a treacherous night into my memory. It all began with a profound feeling, an emotion. I was determined to make a gesture, to show her that my feelings were genuine, that she was someone I hold close to my heart.

It was time to become more committed to our relationship. Too young to ask for her hand in marriage, I wanted her to know how much she meant to me. I could not imagine my world without her and how our parents would try to separate us if they knew how deeply in love I was with her. My love for her was pure and unwavering in making a vow to her.

However destiny had other plans for me that fateful afternoon. It wasn't all smooth sailing. Her stern and protective father would have killed me if he had known my thoughts about his little girl. Not just for asking her to marry me but for taking her away from the towne she grew up in. Little did he know what would happen many years later.

Yes, I was actually in love with her. I wanted to be with her forever. But jealousy would be my Achilles' heel in our relationship. We have been dating for months, but it didn't mean we were without disagreements. Jealousy would occasionally rear its ugly head up when we went out.

Being as beautiful as she was, she would often draw attention from other boys. I would get tangled in my thoughts when we went out, and boys would just say, *'hi'* to her. The green-eyed monster of jealousy would rear its head, making my heart race and my mind spiral to undo me.

This jealousy issue was a big block in our relationship. I couldn't shake the feeling that she was too pretty for dating someone like me. In my mind, I imagined other guys lurking, waiting for me to leave so they could ask her out. I knew this irrational fear had to stop. But I never realized she went out with me because she wanted to.

My mind was always on the wrong side of where it should have been when I saw her talking to other boys. I realized I could not smother her with jealousy, but I did, as I did not know how to control it.

I lacked confidence in myself being with her. She is out of my league, as I was told by so people many from work. What was I supposed to do? The jealousy had to stop!

One afternoon after school, I found myself in front of a jewelry store, wanting to do something special. I decided to go in and look around for a plain and simple gift. Something to make up for my jealous moods that she has tolerated. I initially considered a charm bracelet guided by a friendly saleswoman towards a different idea- a friendship ring.

'A friendship ring?' I said. She began to explain the ring.

'it would symbolize your commitment to her. It means you support her and her thoughts, and your friendship never dies; your love lives on no matter what happens between you, it will endure.'

She continued to share her story of receiving a friendship ring in high school and how she and her friend have remained close even though they had married other people. The idea resonated with me. I wanted to marry her, and this ring could be the perfect way to convey my commitment to her without putting pressure on our young shoulders.

On the crisp autumn day, the saleswoman led me to the ring section, where a glimmering collection of Friendship Rings awaited. Among those treasures, she unveiled a captivating friendship ring adorned with a deep, mystical hue of topaz, Pam's birthstone. Its shimmering facets held the promise of an unspoken connection between us, a silent testament to our bond. In 1967, teenage love was often painted with innocence and fervor, much like the whirlwind of emotions I found myself entangled in. As I envisioned that ring gracing her delicate finger, it seemed like a beacon of hope, a talisman to quell the tumultuous waves of jealousy tormenting my heart. Perhaps this gesture, in the language of teenage love, would be the key to steadying the roller coaster of emotions between us.

I decided to seize the opportunity and purchased the ring, envisioning the delight in her eyes when she receives it.

The ring cost me twenty or thirty dollars, but I was only making a dollar twenty-five an hour at the store, and layaway would be the only way I could own it. I finished the paperwork for the ring purchase and then gave my first payment of five dollars. I was beaming with pride and joy. I couldn't wait to pay for it and place it on her finger.

Over the next few weeks, I made my payments diligently. Finally, the day arrived when I could make the final payment. The saleswoman brought out the ring, showed it to me, then placed it in the ring box and wrapped it up as if it were a birthday or Christmas gift. I couldn't help but smile as she wrapped it. I felt the warmth of the gift that would express my love and commitment to her.

On a slightly chilly mid-October day, the afternoon was adorned with the vibrant colors of autumn, the trees resplendent with fiery hues, and the air crisp with a chill that should have only enhanced the moment. But, little did I know, an insidious seed of insecurity had already taken root in my heart.

I called her one afternoon after school and asked if I could come by. I made my way to the house, ring in hand. When I arrived, her mother welcomed me at the door, and just as she did, Pam grabbed a light jacket and said, *'Let's take a walk around the neighborhood.'* Pam, ready for a walk, joined me.

During our time together, I found myself struggling with feelings of jealousy, particularly when it came to other boys showing interest in Pam. Memories of past encounters where the older boys flirted with Pam triggered a wave of insecurity and jealousy within me. As I stood there looking at her with the ring in my hand. My inability to control these emotions led to a tense argument between us.

My jealousy escalated, and I reacted impulsively out of a combination of fear and frustration. I expressed my distress to her by tossing away the friendship ring in a fit of anger, a regrettable action driven by the overwhelming emotions I was feeling.

As I watched that ring box fly down the street and land in a pile of leaves, I deeply regretted allowing my jealousy to manifest in such a harmful way. I realized then that my inability to manage these emotions had a detrimental impact on our relationship, creating unnecessary conflict and tension. It was never about Pam's actions or intentions; it was about my struggle to trust and feel secure in my relationship with her.

But when she asked what it was that I tossed down the road into a pile of leaves, I told her it was her friendship ring.

'My what?' she said.

'Your friendship ring that I wanted to give to you today.'

'Why did you throw it in the leaves?'

'I thought you were the one for me, but now I wonder if I was wrong!'

She rushed down the street, fueled by a surge of jealousy, straight to the pile of leaves. Frantically, she scattered them in every direction, desperately sifting through, searching for that tiny box holding the cherished ring. Yet despite her efforts, the elusive item remained hidden. Frustration and anger consumed her as she stormed back home, her back rigid and unmoving, refusing to cast a glance in my direction. Silently, I trailed behind her, an uneasy silence lingering between us.

Reaching her doorstep, she marched onto the porch, forcefully slamming the door shut behind her. Standing on the sidewalk, I couldn't help but stare at the closed door, uncertainty filling the air. Minutes ticked by with no sign of Pam emerging. With a final glance at the door, a sense of resignation settled in. Slowly, I turned away, retreating to the car and departing, leaving her behind in the wake of our unresolved turmoil.

Regret washed over me like a cold wave, and I realized that my actions had damaged our budding relationship irreparably. I had let my insecurities rule my heart. I had cast aside a symbol of friendship and affection that I had hoped would have conveyed my feelings to her. It was an afternoon I would never forget, an afternoon when my doubts and fears had led to the loss of something precious, lost in the depths of the gutter and in the depths of my own self-doubt.

Our relationship ended that day, and we went our separate ways. I couldn't control my jealousy, and it had cost me the love of my life. Pam had given me many chances to overcome it, but I failed.

Even though we were no longer together, I could not stop thinking of her. I often drove by her house, hoping for a glimpse of her or any clue about her life, but I never saw her with anyone else.

I had never had such a rage before, but that day, there was a rage I would forever regret. I couldn't control my suspicions. I was so possessive while dating her. I wanted her all to myself, and nobody else could have her. Most of my anger was over suspicion of her. It was an unfortunate part of my teenage years.

My unrelenting lack of confidence and self-trust greatly impacted my high school dating experiences, causing strain in all my future relationships. Coping with the loss of Pam during my senior year was incredibly challenging, a struggle that persisted even as I prepared to enlist in the military.

Now that Pam and I were no longer going out, I left my position at D'Amatos and found work in Brockton, selling shoes for Thom McAn at the Westgate Mall. Working at the same store as Pam would just bring unfathomable heartbreak.

Despite my efforts, her presence lingered persistently in my thoughts. I grappled through school, diligently attending summer classes to compensate for distraction, diverting my attention from my studies.

One day, I heard that Pam had left her job at D'Amatos. She had moved on. But the memory of the friendship ring I had tossed away haunted me for many years.

Return from Vietnam 1972
New Chapter of Life

After my second tour in Vietnam concluded, I finally stepped onto home soil- a place obscured from my view for four long years. May 5, 1972, marked my return to my beloved hometown in Massachusetts. Swiftly, by May 7th of the same year, I reintegrated into the familiar halls of Halliday's, the printing and bindery company where I once was a full-time employee before military service. However, the landscape had shifted. Instead of resuming my former post at the folding machine in the bindery, a role I'd left behind, I was offered a position on the second shift at the Hanover plant as a janitor. The contrast was stark, a departure from my former duties, yet I stood poised to embrace this new chapter of civilian life.

To say I was disappointed would be an understatement. After four years of working on multi-million dollar aircraft and assuming leadership responsibilities, I found myself in charge of little more than a broom and a two-dollar piece of equipment, responsible for cleaning up after those who couldn't. It was, to say, less than humbling and embarrassing experience as I believe this position did not truly reflect my capabilities.

My spirit grew increasingly disheartened as I toiled away at my janitorial job. Occasionally, they would whisk me into the bustling printing room. Yet, my newfound knowledge was limited to the art of applying ink to the rollers. The allure of attending FAA school at East Coast Aero Tech beckoned. Still, memories of my former high school sweetheart, Pam, resurfaced as my mind wandered. She was the girl I had fallen head over heels for, and her image loomed large during long work nights.

My thoughts were consumed by her, overshadowing the mundane tasks of sweeping and cleaning those unsavory ashtrays filled with discarded cigarette butts. I found myself reminiscing about the last time I saw her, working diligently at the supermarket where her father was employed. Questions filled my mind: Is she still there? Was she available for a potential reunion?

My high school friend, Al, worked in construction, setting up modular homes for a new retirement community in Halifax. Knowing how much I disliked my current job, he offered to help me get a job with his company.

I disliked sweeping and operating on the second shift. Had my former employer put me back on at the bindery factory, I might have stayed, but I'm not sweeping and picking up after people. The Air Force didn't spend all that taxpayer's money on my training just to have me become an entry-level employee.

I took Al's offer and was hired by the construction company. I installed skirting around the new homes and fixed minor problems as they arose. The Korean War veteran business owner had no issue with my military background. I enjoyed the job and the opportunity to use my hands and brain daily. However, I was still not happy. I couldn't find what truly made me happy. I kept missing the Air Force and the friends I had made. Most of all, I missed working on aircraft.

As work became more disparaging, I debated going to FAA school at East Coast Aero Tech. And thoughts of my old high school sweetheart Pam kept returning to my mind. I recalled last seeing her working at the supermarket in Randolph and wondered if she might still be there. Or was she available to date?

Al, my closest friend from high school, was now in the United States Navy Reserves and was leaving for his annual summer active duty training, leaving me without any friends.

Al and I were different now than when we were friends in high school. Our personalities have changed over the past four years. We had drifted from being close friends the dynamics of our friendship had changed since our high school days.

With Al away, I decided to find out if Pam, my former girlfriend, was still in town and where she worked. One evening after work, I drove to Pam's parent's house for a surprise visit. I knocked on the door, and her mother answered. I said, *'hello'* and asked her if she might have remembered me. She was unsure who I was but said I looked familiar to her. I told her who I was. That was when she said she remembered me from when I dated Pam. She was excited to see me. Mrs. 'B.' invited me in. Pam's dad was in the next room and only said hello. But Mrs. B and I talked for what seemed to be hours as we sat in the kitchen.

After about an hour of talking about where I've been and what I did in the Air Force and catching her up on my life, Mrs. B. had a surprise for me about Pam.

Mrs. B spoke enthusiastically about Pam's life. All I heard in my head was the Charlie Brown character talking blah blah blah, followed by

'Pam is married.'

How could she be married? I kept hearing it in my head. Why? Then, thoughts of our time together came to my mind. Edaville Railroad, Duxbury, and Lincoln Park were all places we loved, especially Edaville Railroad; we fell in love there. Mrs. B continued to speak; she told me more about Pam's marriage, where she is, and what her husband does in the military. I wanted to get up and leave.

However, I did not want to be rude as she seemed thrilled about talking about Pam and what she had done with her life.

'Helen,' I said, *'that's wonderful about Pam, but I've overkept my stay.'*

Then she said Pam would be calling this coming Sunday. She stated they had their weekly calls each Sunday as the cost of long-distance was less on Sunday, and she invited me back to the house so I could say hello to her.

'Come back Sunday evening, Bob, around seven p.m.,' she said.

'Pam will be surprised you came to see her and say hello.'

These were her final words to me as I left her home. You're not kidding; she'll be surprised, I thought. That's an understatement.

Sunday is a long way off, and I wasn't sure I wanted to return, but what could it hurt just to say hello to her? The answer to the question was a lot!

Sunday evening came, and I drove back to her mother's house just before seven. And again, like before, I was invited in with her mother's open arms. We again sat at the kitchen table near the wall phone. She told me Pam would be calling this week, so we sat and talked while we waited for the phone to ring.

Then the phone rang, and I got a little nervous. Mrs. B got up from her chair and answered the phone. After her mother finished speaking with her, she spoke with her dad in a short conversation. Then the phone went back to Mrs. B when I heard her say to Pam.

'there is someone from your past here in my kitchen sitting with me that you might like to say hello to as you knew him very well,'

She was piquing Pam's interest. I was then given the phone. As I took the phone from Mrs. B, I grew very nervous and unsettled. My voice cracked as I thanked her. I held the phone in my hand away from my face and was ready to give the phone back to her. But then, for some reason, I raised the phone to my face and said hello. She knew instantly who it was.

I had been out of her life for over four years, and she still recognized my voice. I'm talking to Pam, and while doing so, I see her in my mind; I'm seeing the girl I loved back in high school. While we talked, I realized how much I loved her back then. I recalled the hurt when I last saw her at the grocery store in Randolph. I walked out of the store, thinking, what a fool I had been back then. And what it was to have caused me to have left her?

As we were speaking, I realized now that she was the one I was in love with. And now I wanted to be with her.

It felt like yesteryears when we dated and laughed as we spoke to one another on the phone. In our conversation, she mentioned coming home to bring her son back to visit her mom and dad. She asked me if I could come by and meet with her and see her son. She was so proud of her son; I could hear it in her voice. I said I would love to. Then I thought, '*Why?*' I never thought anything would come from that invitation. But when she came home, things would change for both of us.

All the while this was happening, I had started reentry back into the Air Force. I missed the comradery I had while in the service. Since I've been out, I found myself drinking more and having more depression while living at home. I thought I needed a more structured life than what I have. In the Air Force, the experience was different. I was given so much responsibility and had more friends than now. I enjoyed my career field in aircraft maintenance and the traveling that went with it.

A week passed, and Pam arrived home to her parents. I called her, and we talked for an hour that first night; we had much to cover from our past. I could feel I was falling in love with her all over again. Then she invited me over to her parents' house.

How stupid I was to do what I did when she came home. I knew I was still immature as I wanted to be with her. We would keep visiting each other the week she was home. Her mother was good with us going out as friends. We would go to an old place where we often spent time,

Papa Ginos. We just sat, ate pizza, and laughed at the times we spent there as we dated.

While there, memories were re-lived, and we had a great time as if she wasn't married. Just carrying on as two teenagers, we weren't. But I didn't let that stop me. We had our pizza and then traveled back through DW Field Park, a place we would go to as teenagers and make out. While we drove through the park, we encountered the old stone castle where we used to run up the stairs to the top and overlook the area. In the winter, we would slide down the snow-covered hill in front of the stone castle. We entered this stone building, and the smell of urine was terrible, and the stairs were now blocked off for use. Still, we laughed and talked about those teen years like they were yesterday. We returned to the car and searched for places we knew we had made out. Then one of the places came into view, and I pulled the car into the spot. We talked a little about this place, and then I kissed her. She didn't try to stop me. Could it be she, too, was still in love with me?

After the kiss, nothing was said; we continued to talk and laugh about those places we went and the time we spent together during those carefree days as teenagers. It was when I knew I was still in love with her and told her. Our conversation got quiet. Pam sat back and began with,

'Remember when,'

And that's all she had to say. From there, I did remember what it was that we did that night. I didn't care if she was married; I wanted her. She wrapped her arms around my neck to keep our lips together.

'Pam,' was all I said!

Then we just sat at Field Park until the police came by and told us to leave. It was just like high school. I took her home and walked her to the front porch. It was just about 11 p.m., and we said our good nights.

But it didn't end there; she wanted to get together again, and I was too happy to say yes. Whatever she wanted, I wanted.

While she was home, I continued to search for better employment. I now wanted to keep from returning to the military, but I could not find any work that would make me happy as the military did. I went to East Coast Aero Tech to see if I could be accepted into the next class for my A&P license. I was accepted and would begin the next class, which was in September. But September seemed like an eternity away, even though it was only two weeks.

Not much time passed between Pam and me when my visit started to cause trouble in her family. I would be taking her out, along with her son, and we would spend overnights together while I drove to New Hampshire in search of work. We spent a night or two in Portsmouth, New Hampshire, and stayed in a motel with cabin cottages. The place had no baby beds, so Pam made one using the dresser drawers and placed blankets in it for her son. The following day, we drove to Manchester, where I would try to find a position with the New Hampshire National Guard as a helicopter mechanic.

After Manchester, we drove back to Portsmouth Naval Station to see if any opportunities were available at the shipyard. I applied to any open positions they had, but nothing came from it. No calls came from my searches, and I grew even more disappointed with my finding employment to take care of Pam and her son. I didn't want her to leave and go back to North Dakota.

Still, I had been waiting for a slot to reenter the Air Force. I'm unsure Pam knew about this until I received my enlistment authorization. I could have gone to the Air Force Reserves and applied for an ARTS (air reserve technician) position had I known about those openings. There were several in Westover Air Force Reserve Base. They had C-130s at that base. This would have accomplished what I needed without us leaving Massachusetts.

I would try a couple more places to work. Being hired to work at Boston Whaler in Rockland was my last and final try to stay home. I could work evenings there and attend days at East Coast Aero Tech for my training for my FAA license. Pam drove me to the factory on my first day at work. When she arrived back to pick me up that evening, it was my last day at that factory. I could not do that type of work after being an aircraft mechanic.

I finally told Pam I would return to the military as I felt it was best for me. I never asked her how she felt about me returning to active duty, nor caring enough to talk to her about it. For all her goodness, Pam accepted all of my bad decisions. Now I've placed her in a position of choosing between me, her marriage, and her family. She decided to come with me to my new base in Tucson, Arizona. And for that, I was so ever grateful. I knew she could have said no, and I would have been heartbroken.

Leaving for Arizona

I took the Oath of Enlistment for the Air Force on October 10, 1972. Pam was at her mother's house during my re-enlistment. Soon after I raised my hand and pledged to defend the United States Constitution, I received my orders to report to the 100th OMS (Operational Maintenace Squadron) at Davis-Monthan Air Force Base, Tucson, Arizona, on October 18th, 1972. I am officially a blue suiter again, and I feel much better knowing I am back working on C-130s.

I do not recall conversations with Pam before my re-enlistment in the military. She knew how miserable I was with the civilian world and that I was in the process of returning to active duty. But she did not get a say in what I was about to do.

After re-enlisting, I again asked Pam if she wanted to stay with me and move to Arizona. As much as I loved her, I would understand if she did not want to drive twenty-six hundred miles away from home and start a new life. But she decided she wanted to be with me, and I was glad she did. Now she had to break the news to her parents.

As Pam visited her with her mother, I went to Hanscom Air Force Base, collecting my military and travel pay for the trip to Arizona. The next day we rented a rooftop carrier and loaded up the 1968 Barracuda with just as much as we could with items we would need, mainly clothes. We gathered in the Barracuda the next day and left Massachusetts, heading west.

Somewhere before we arrived in Tucson, maybe during our travel, regrets may have entered Pam's mind, or perhaps she began to have different feelings about living far away from her home. Pam was quiet during the drive to Tucson but didn't seem unhappy.

Road trip and New Mexico

Our drive towards the west consisted of long days of riding in the car with few stops. Air Force regulations for PCS travel were that you travel no more than 350 miles or 8 hours behind the wheel. We spent ten to twelve hours a day in the car, with necessary stops for food and relief. We would combine the food and comfort stops with our refuel stops.

Most of the ride in the Barracuda was comfortable until we crossed the panhandle of Texas into New Mexico. Once we ventured the southern route through New Mexico to connect to the interstate I-10, the ride grew increasingly warmer inside the car. The Barracuda had no air conditioning. Why would I need it? I purchased the vehicle in Massachusetts.

When we stopped for the evening to spend the night at a motel, Pam would call home to let her mother know she was okay. I never thought Pam might not be happy with her decision, and if so, she had concealed those feelings well during our trip. All I could do was let her know that I hoped to make it better for her when we arrived in Arizona.

Each day passed, and we inched closer to the mysterious heart of Arizona. On one fateful evening, during a seemingly endless drive that had stretched well into the darkest hours, exhaustion began to gnaw at my bones. The desolated stretch of I-40 offered no respite in the form of motels, leaving us with no choice but to continue on, weary and disoriented.

In the distance, an ominous silhouette loomed ahead, a refuge shrouded in shadows, beckoning us with an air of desolation. Our location remained a haunting enigma, a place lost in time and space.

As I pulled the car into this unknown territory that seemed to be a rest stop, a sense of foreboding crept over us.

Pam and I huddled over the map, tracing an uncertain path to find we had ventured west of Amarillo, Texas, and now found ourselves stranded somewhere in the desolate heart of New Mexico. The area we occupied was just wide enough for our car to find sanctuary, cloaked in the inky blackness. The occasional vehicles that passed by were phantoms, assuring us that this sinister spot could serve as our temporary refuge.

Pam painstakingly arranged heavy coats from the back seat, transforming the cramped area into a makeshift sanctuary. The night's frigid embrace had descended upon us, casting a chill that bit through our bones. We clung to the hope of finding solace in this strange, isolated haven, seeking shelter from the impending darkness.

We surrendered to the weariness that clung to our sinister specter, permitting ourselves a few moments of sleep. The world outside these glass windows remained still, a spectral desert of uncertainty.

But just as we were on the precipice of slumber, a deafening wail split the silence, piercing the night's fragile tranquility. It was 4:00 a.m., and I jolted upright, my heart pounding. My gaze fixated upon the source of the cacophonous intrusion – a colossal train, an unexpected sentinel of doom. Unbeknownst to us, we had unwittingly parked beside a treacherous train crossing, trapped with no escape.

The train's colossal headlight swung from side to side, illuminating the window's interior as the mechanical behemoth roared past. All we could see were the relentless wheels of the engine, and the haunting clickety–clack of the train cars haunted our senses for an eternity.

In our weariness, we had unknowingly invited this surreal nightmare into our lives. The space had only permitted us to park parallel to the unseen tracks, devoid of any warning signs or safety measures.

Was this another divine intervention, or had we inadvertently stumbled into a sinister twist of fate? The enigma deepened as we clung to the desperate hope that we would somehow emerge from this ordeal unscathed.

Pam and I were now fully awake from that scare and the train ahead of us; we decided to continue driving for the day to take advantage of the cooler air as we crossed New Mexico.

Pam moved the coats from the centre console to her side door for well-deserved sleep before sunrise and the day getting hot. I drove towards Hollomon Air Force Base, hoping we could get a night's lodging.

We came upon another road outside Santa Rosa, New Mexico, with signage to the town where Holloman Air Force Base was. Our destination for this day. Stopped to review the map, Pam noticed we could take a road to where we wanted to go. It was a state road, not the interstate. We planned to go into Albuquerque and down and cross towards Holloman Air Base. We knew continuing to use the interstate would allow access to gas stations, cafes, and bathrooms. Pam thought we should take the secondary road as it would bring us directly to Holloman Air Force Base. She noticed that it was shorter than our original travel plans.

Holloman's stay was our original plan of spending several nights there. We agreed to take that road that would bring us to the base and hoped we could get there with the fuel we had left and that, if needed, there was another service station along the way.

We had no problem taking the short route. There were several service stations along the way, and we found its scenery beautiful. We had plenty of gas in the Barracuda by taking Pam's suggested route.

Pam's plan was right; we made it to Holloman Air Force Base in the early afternoon, drove to base lodging, and asked if we could get two days in temporary housing. We have been traveling for 4 days almost nonstop, with only a couple motel stops. We needed a place to get a good night's rest, not to mention a shower and fresh laundry.

After we settled in, Pam made sure she called her mother and told her she was fine and where she was. That evening, after we washed all our dirty laundry, we returned to our room and relaxed on the two chairs on the small stoop in front of our room.

What a different feeling the night had here in the southwest. Here it is, mid-October, and seventy degrees at 8 p.m. We were sitting outside our room without jackets on, looking into the night sky and saying to each other how much closer the stars seemed to be to us than they were back in Massachusetts. As I reached for her hand to hold, we turned to each other and smiled.

Desert Love

Under the vast desert sky, we gazed up at the celestial tapestry. In that serene moment, we witnessed shooting stars streaking across the night canvas, seemingly choreographed for our viewing pleasure. We continued looking up at the stars as we savored this enchanting cosmic display; we couldn't help but feel connected to the Earth's gentle rotation. It was as though we were drifting through the universe with the stars as our guide. The night deepened, and the stillness around us took on an almost mystical quality, allowing us to hear distant whispers and faint sounds carried on the breeze. The enigmatic night sounds sparkled our imaginations with wild fantasies, prompting us to retreat to the safety of our room, where our love story continued in hushed whispers, unspoken yet deeply felt.

After our second night, we rose up early, aiming to depart for Tucson before the sun's scorching embrace could reach us on the road. Before our departure, we made a pit stop at the commissary, grabbing some snacks for our journey. Little did we anticipate that a seemingly innocent selection of fruit would lead to an unexpected encounter with the Arizona vigilant agricultural authorities. We found ourselves face to face with the fruit police, an amusing twist in our adventure. To cross the Arizona state line, we had to make a choice: consume our fruity contraband or bid it farewell. I chose to savor the fruit, and with that quirky encounter behind us, we continued on our way. Our hearts are lighter as we approach our final travel day.

Our journey's final leg presented us with a challenge: a car lacking air-conditioning amid rising desert temperatures. Dressed in cool shorts and short sleeves, Pam sat beside me, an embodiment of grace in her summer attire. Her hair danced in the wind, and her hand gracefully brushed away the errant strands as we ventured toward our ultimate destination. The relentless road noise made our conversation and radio listening difficult. Still, the presence of Pam by my side made such trivialities inconsequential. She was my Venus, and I couldn't have been more grateful for her company on this scorching yet love-filled journey.

Arriving in Tucson

We reached Tucson in just four hours after departing Holloman Air Force Base. As we drove through the base's front gate, security police personnel provided us with clear directions to the guest lodging.

Being part of the military has its perks, and one of them is the affordable accommodations available to traveling airmen on various bases. Our assigned room was at the end of the second-floor hallway, and we would call it home for the next week. It resembled a coy one-bedroom efficiency, offering us a comfortable retreat.

This marked a significant change from our previous travels, where we often found ourselves in roadside motels devoid of air conditioning. Here, we were greeted by the welcoming embrace of a well-cooled room, a small luxury that made our stay all the more enjoyable.

FROM THE COLLECTION OF BOB CROTHERS D-M BILLETING

Arriving at the new base, we found ourselves navigating a sea of novelty. Among the myriad adjustments, the most noticeable was the shift in time. When Pam reached out to family back home, she had to meticulously factor in the time difference. Adding three hours to her calls became a daily ritual, a conscious effort to synchronize with the time in our hometown. Consequently, reaching out to the East Coast required early-day conversations.

Our TV-watching habits also transformed. Shows that once graced our screens at 8:00 p.m. back home now aired at 7:00p.m. in the Mountain Time Zone. Watching programs that used to accompany our evenings now brighten our late afternoons felt peculiar. Everything began a bit earlier and wrapped up sooner. The late news, once delivered at 11:00p.m., now arrived promptly at 10:00p.m.

One significant aspect of Arizona's living was that time remained constant, unmoved by the whims of daylight saving time. There was no "spring ahead" or "falling back." Time simply flowed steadily, a steady anchor in our lives.

Amidst all these changes, Pam stood as my unwavering source of comfort and stability. She was not just my partner but my rock, the cornerstone of our shared journey. Her presence infused our experiences with a sense of rightness. Life felt better with her by my side, and no matter how challenging, our journey felt destined for happiness.

Now that we were all checked in, we could finally enjoy a restful first night. Saturday arrived, and luckily, there were no immediate responsibilities like reporting to my new unit or finding central base personnel. So, we decided to explore the base. The mild weather was a pleasant surprise, so we began our stroll around the lodging area. My main objective was to locate the CPBO building, as I needed to sign in on Mon day. Along the way, we stumbled upon the base exchange and commissary.

When Monday arrived, it was time to don my military uniform and start the processing for the base and my unit. This left Pam with the significant task of finding a place to live. Without her assistance, we wouldn't have had a place to call home, especially considering I had to report to my new squadron the next day. That first week would have been a disaster without Pam's invaluable support.

Pam's Invaluable Assistance

Pam, our savior in a new and unfamiliar city, led us to a cozy haven in Tucson, nestled near the University of Arizona. She transformed our initial dingy apartment into a place we wholeheartedly called home during our brief stay. Without her, we might have resorted to living out of our car.

Our journey began when Pam struck up a friendship with an officer's wife while we were staying in base lodging. This newfound friend informed Pam about a rental unit she and her husband owned, conveniently located near the university and the base. It was a two-bedroom gem they were willing to rent to us, and Pam eagerly checked it out in person while I was at work.

The apartment had just become available, and we were more than ready to make it our new abode. It was a charming townhouse with tasteful furnishings that exuded a delightful southwestern flair. I vividly recall our initial visit together, where the unit felt somewhat barren, its emptiness accentuated by the sparse furniture. Nevertheless, we needed to vacate the base lodging soon, and this place would serve as our interim haven. In no time, we moved in, even before our week in base lodging came to an end.

Apparently, this heater failed to provide warmth to any room except for the kitchen, where the gas stove offered some respite from the cold. The back bedrooms remained perpetually chilly and drafty, yet we somehow found a way to tolerate these harsh living conditions. It served as a temporary abode until we could secure a more suitable place to call home.

Finding a Second Job and Exploring Tucson

I applied at Ryan Airfield outside Tucson and was hired as a sheet metal worker on a DC-3 aircraft. The field was just southwest of where we lived. Ryan Airfield was built by the United States Army Air Forces in 1942 as a site for primary flight training. It was part of many Arizona World War II Army Airfields. Military flight training at Ryan ceased in 1944, and the property was conveyed to the State of Arizona in 1948.

The company I worked for remodeled the old military C-47s and DC-3s. I work from 7:00 a.m. to 2:00 p.m. After leaving my first job, I would return to our apartment, change into my uniform, go to my unit on base, and work from 4:00 p.m. to midnight. As difficult as it was for me to do this, the second job was necessary to help pay for the rent, food, and other things; however, it seemed to cost us more in our relationship than I received for working.

While working at the base, Pam often waited for my return home every night. She was tired, and I could see how difficult things were for her being here; she had no transportation as I had to use the car to travel to both jobs. Those late nights were our only time to talk about her day during the week. My time spent with Pam was very short with our arrival in Tucson.

Soon, Pam became friends with an elderly lady several doors down from us. They would spend time together while I worked. And it seemed they had become good friends.

Pam and I would discover Tucson on weekends when I was not performing weekend duty on the base. We traveled all over the city, finding our way around. There was this one place out on the far east side called Pinnacle Peak. It was a western tourist town; its fame was this old-style saloon and restaurant. They had steak dinners, but what made them unique were the ties hanging from the ceiling in the restaurant. Hundreds of them! The story was that if you came in with a necktie, they would cut it off and hang it from the rafters above. One night, we had dinner there. We heard a loud bell ringing as we sat and waited for our meal. Pam and I turned and looked as we saw people with neckties on. Later, our friends told us that most people visiting for the winter would wear ties just to have this happen to them. We saw this place twice, once by ourselves and another with our friends Duane and Sally. I worked with Duane on the base.

We were driving around when we came upon a store named Goldwaters. How odd it was to see that name as a Senator from Arizona had that name. Found out later there is a reason for the Goldwater store. We went to the mall, which was large and beautiful compared to those in Massachusetts. It was vast, with many unknown store names to both of us.

Another weekend, we traveled out to explore the town again. We went to a movie set called 'Old Tucson' this time. The movie set was far from the city limits, situated on the west side of downtown Tucson. We were excited to see an actual movie set and see what TV shows we used to watch as kids and what our parents watched, which were made at this studio. We were in awe as we stood in the exact location of Ricky Nelson in the movie *Rio Bravo*. In another studio part, we toured the TV show *High Chaparral*. It was fascinating to see all the buildings we remembered from those TV and movies in a remote studio location.

While walking around the studio, we talked about how close all the buildings were but how they seemed so far away on the show. As they say, the magic of TV and movies gives us the illusion of something being in the distance and not on the set.

Every building was close to another building. We spent so much time on the back lots, reminiscing what we knew from seeing them in the movies or on TV, that we didn't get to the sound stage. We would have to return another time for that tour; that time never happened.

Operation Linebacker II
Christmas War

Shortly after arriving at Davis-Monthan, I was notified that I would leave for a TDY. Msgt. Fredrick had requested that I be sent over to U-Tapao for this operation. We had been stationed in Vietnam, and he knew of my skills as a crew chief.

Pam and I had to quickly get our lives in order. My TDY for an unknown number of days was coming soon, and I would leave no matter what was or was not completed.

I embarked on this TDY (Temporary Duty Assignment) due to the conclusion of the Paris Peace talks and the subsequent escalation of the bombing campaigns in North Vietnam by the President. Our aircraft played a pivotal role in supporting these bombing missions, which were set to continue until the North Vietnamese returned to the negotiation table. Specifically, our drones were tasked with capturing imagery of the bombing areas, which would then be relayed to intelligence for analysis and assessment.

I was one of many crew chiefs on the DC-130A/E aircraft in the 100SRW. Each plane flew drones under its wings. The aircraft I work on carried two drones on an outer pylon. The DC-130Es spent the majority of their time in Thailand. Our other aircraft, the DC-130As, spent most of their time in Osan, Korea.

A DC-130E could upload two drones under its wing, and we had external fuel tanks for the extended range of the aircraft. Each mission would involve the planes flying north, taking our aircraft toward north Vietnam; they would cross over Cambodia and Laos and back into

Vietnam on some missions. They may have even crossed into North Vietnam; no one ever spoke of that if we had or had not!

FROM THE COLLECTION OF BOB CROTHERS DC-130E

The DC-130E carried 6 Officers and 2 enlisted members on missions. The flight crew consisted of a pilot, co-pilot, flight engineer, and navigator. A booth housed those who tended the drones in the specialized compartment behind bulkhead 245. It would be 1 RCO (remote control officer), 2 LCO (launch control officers), one for each drone carried on the aircraft, and 1 ART (airborne radar technician). Once the drones were launched by the LCO, they remained in orbit, controlled by the RCO, and tracked by the ART until their mission was complete. Upon the mission's completion, A specially outfitted CH-53 equipped with an aerial recovery system would snag the drone mid-air after it popped its recovery chute. The capture of this drone was critical due to the contents of the camera and its mission. Once the helio captured the drone, it would fly back to Nakhon Phanom, also known as NKP or Naked Fanny, 75 miles from the North Vietnam border, on the 17th parallel, and a short driving distance of 235 miles to downtown Hanoi. Our DC-130 would fly ahead to NKP, land, and await the drone's return. It would be uploaded onto the aircraft, flown back to U-Tapao Air Base, and ready for another mission on another day.

Early morning Drone mission

1. Looking towards the front, you can see two radar domes. The first dome in the front of the aircraft is the aircraft radar. The bottom dome is to track the drones once launched.
2. The drone in the picture is being prepared for its mission. All the electronics are located in this section of the drone.
3. Behind that black tail cone on the drone is a parachute that will be extracted once the recovery helicopter is nearby after the mission.
4. What you can not see are the cameras located in the nose of the drone.

Costly Car Repair Dilemma

As my departure for overseas loomed ever closer, a daunting checklist of tasks clamored for my attention, and chief among them was orchestrating Pam's relocation. The prospect of her remaining in our current abode during my absence was a thought I couldn't bear. Yet, the hurdles before us seemed insurmountable. Our trusty, albeit sweltering, car had succumbed to the relentless demands of the road, necessitating costly repairs. Money was scarce, and the notion of acquiring a new vehicle had never graced our budgetary plans.

Shortly after we departed from the base, our Baracuda experienced a sudden breakdown one fateful afternoon. The front brake line gave way while we were returning to our apartment. In a moment of quick thinking, I relied on the emergency hand brake to maintain control of the car as we cautiously made our way back home.

I scheduled an appointment with the local Plymouth dealer on Monday to address the issue. Fortunately, the dealership was conveniently situated near our residence. However, this predicament left us without any means of transportation. I explained to the service manager the situation's urgency, emphasizing that I needed the car later that day for my base duties. Regrettably, the service manager said the car would be in their possession for the entire day. This unexpected delay made it challenging, particularly regarding my part-time job commitments.

Our financial situation was precarious, with just a meager sum remaining from my second job's earnings and the travel allowance I received for relocating to Tucson. Every penny, nickel, and dime had to be meticulously gathered to cover the steep repair bill. Pam even contributed the funds her mother had given her before we departed.

Lacking a checking account or credit card, we were blindsided by the exorbitant cost of one hundred dollars, a substantial sum for someone in the military, mainly when my monthly income hovered just above that amount. It's entirely possible that this unexpected expense played a role in Pam's decision to seek employment to assist with finances.

Pam Seeking Work

One Sunday morning, following our recent car trouble, Pam made the decision to actively search for employment. She began her quest for work in the vicinity of our apartment. Although I can't recall the exact number of places Pam visited, one particular interview stands out in my memory, and I accompanied her. Since we shared a single car, we embarked on this journey together as she explored potential job opportunities.

Pam informed me about a local furniture store that was in need of someone to assist the owner in their office. She promptly made a call and scheduled an interview.

The evening before Pam's interview, she dedicated time to preparing for it meticulously. She meticulously selected an outfit and sought my opinion on it. It was a remarkable choice! Pam had always possessed a knack for dressing sharply and knew how to make a lasting impression with her attire. I assured her that she looked absolutely stunning and exuded an air of classiness in that outfit. Pam had a remarkable ability to create a gorgeous interview outfit from the clothes she already owned.

Nevertheless, I always found her incredibly attractive no matter what she wore. Sometimes, I had to remind myself that Pam and I were together, as I couldn't believe my luck. I considered myself fortunate to have her by my side, especially during such moments.

Pam and I navigated the early morning streets of Tucson, our destination set for her interview. As we arrived at the location, a quaint storefront emerged before us. Determined, Pam stepped out of the car, a confident smile accentuating her professional attire. I wished her luck as she disappeared into the store, leaving me to wait in the quiet solitude of the car.

As moments stretched into minutes, I took a stroll to alleviate the anticipatory silence. The surroundings hold a tranquil charm. This store was located in an older section of Tucson. The morning light painted everything in a soft golden hue. Each step I took seemed to weave between the passing minutes and the world unfurling around me.

A father and his young child basked in a tender bonding moment near where I stood. The child, brimming with unadulterated joy, revealed in the playfulness of their interactions. The father, a picture of strength and love, lifted the child in the air with effortless grace. Eliciting peals of laughter echoed through the serene morning air. The child's giggles formed of innocence, a pure melody resonating in my soul's depths.

For that brief moment, I became an observer of this intimate portrait, a reminder of the beauty found in life's simple moments. The kind that go unnoticed in the rush of our daily existence.

As Pam's return drew near, I couldn't help but carry that snapshot of familial bliss with me- a gentle reminder that amid life's uncertainties, pockets of pure joy do exist, just waiting to be noticed and cherished.

Job Interview Surprise

After Pam emerged from her interview, I couldn't help but ask how it had gone. She paused, her expression a mix of surprise and discomfort, and mentioned,

'It was surprisingly short.'

As she reached into the backseat of the car, I sensed there was more to the story.

'What happened in there?' I probed gently.

Pam hesitated before sharing her initial excitement for the position she had applied for, only to be caught off guard by the owner's unexpected proposal. He wanted to establish a different kind of relationship,' she disclosed, her enthusiasm replaced by disbelief. As she recounted the job details, it took an unexpected turn when the owner made an unsettling request.

'He *wanted me to be his sugar baby*,' she explained,

Her tone conveys a mix of disbelief and unease.

My shock mirrored Pam's as I sought clarity on the situation.

'A sugar baby?' I asked

I tried to wrap my head around the situation. Pam clarified, explaining the nature of the proposition, leaving us both stunned. Urgently, she requested we leave the place, clearly wanting to distance herself from the uncomfortable encounter. I couldn't help but share her unease and the strong urge to comfort her. Still, respecting Pam's wish, we drove away, leaving an unsettling interview experience behind.

Finding a New Place to Live

The apartment we are living in was okay. But I wanted something better for Pam and closer to the base. We also needed to live within our means. Although owned by a military person, the apartment was slightly more than what we were given to live off base with my monthly stipend. We lived close to the university, and rents were higher than they might have been closer to the base. My goal was to make life better for Pam, not worse. I wanted Pam to have the best I could give her and afford. And to have some money left without a second job.

During one of our drives around exploring Tucson, we found these new apartments off Crawford Road and Twenty-Second Street near the base. We stopped and walked to the rental office to inquire about them. We were told they were taking applications, and they gave us the requirements to live there. All the apartments are rent-controlled. The allotment (single BAQ) we received in my pay would cover the rent. This would allow me more time to spend with Pam. We applied for the spacious apartment and were accepted. Our move-in date was going to be close to Christmas or after. But, before we moved, I received notice that I would be leaving for Thailand with the 99th SRS. An Operation called Linebacker II was going into effect.

Strange Noises in the Night

While living in our first apartment near the university, a mysterious noise was heard outside our bedroom window. Pam's wake nudges me, and using her sweet and endearing voice, I get up and investigate the ruckus outside. Reluctantly, I emerged from the warmth of our covers, dressed, and ventured into the cold night. I have now become an amateur detective.

The chilling gust of wind whisked by me, and with it, it brought me back to Vietnam, evoking memories of haunting nocturnal sounds on the flight line when the night air was stilled. Sounds carried for what seemed like miles. Things heard that were not there. The imagination runs wild. Where were their origins? All elusive and unsettling. Amidst that cold air, it also recalled a Massachusetts winter day. Another gust of wind had just come up as I continued my search. Determine, I scoured the surroundings, reminiscent of those tense nights in Vietnam when enigmatic noises echoed around me while I was working on my aircraft shrouded in darkness. As I grappled with the noise, vivid recollections filled my mind. I stumbled around, hunting for the source of the commotion that had awakened the love of my life. As I listened and followed the noise, more thoughts of a time earlier came to mind: Vietnam. By the way, what rule says it's the man's job to investigate noises?

The wind started to blow a little more robust, and with each gust, I got closer to finding the noise. Continuing my search and destroy operation, I moved nearer to the window of the bedroom.

I noticed several branches from the bush planted beneath that window. There was another gust of wind, and I saw those branches move under our bedroom window alongside the outside wall. Hearing it, it sounded like someone was scratching the exterior wall. The longer brush branches caused the problem, so I removed them.

With that now solved, I returned to report my findings to Pam, only to find her safe, warm, and asleep. I hope she feels safer now that I have lost my ability to fall back to sleep. I was fully awake. It would be a very long day for me.

Purchasing New Furniture

After the harrowing night of playing detective, we set off to buy new furniture for the new apartment. We drove to the local WT Grants and went on a shopping spree. We purchased everything we would need to be able to live in that new apartment. We bought a couch, chairs, kitchen table with chairs, two-bedroom sets, one for Pam and me, and one for the second bedroom, with our final purchase of a new stereo console complete with turn table, AM, and FM radio with a headphone connection. Everything was now purchased on a payment plan, scheduled for delivery. It would be delivered to the new apartment on the move-in date.

FROM THE COLLECTION OF BOB CROTHERS-APARTMENT #2

Since our new apartment would not be ready to move in until after I was gone, how would I get Pam moved? My time was coming up fast to leave, and I was worried about the move. My senior supervisor called me into his office and assigned Technical Sergeant Henke as Pam's sponsor while I was away on TDY. He assured me that some men from the unit would be available to help Pam move into the new apartment while I was gone. Technical Sergeant Hinke was Pam's primary contact while I was TDY. If she needed help, she had to call him. But we still had another problem, and that was the Credit Union. The credit union would not allow me to add Pam to the account because we were unmarried. They were strict about who could and could not be placed on my account.

Unrelated persons were not allowed to be added to the account. This ensured that an unrelated person could not just take the money and run off or change arrangements, leaving the service member with no income. Thus, the only way for her to be added was that we would have to be married. And the proof was in the form of a marriage certificate. We tried to say we were married. But on a second try, we were in trouble after we were refused on the first!

Without Pam's access to the checking account and the necessary power of attorney, she had no way to send money. The credit union said that no power of attorney would be given to her without us being married.

Being young, we often put no worries ahead of stupidity. If I had not been ordered to this TDY and had the one year before my rotation, we may have gotten her the needed divorce first. But we did not have time to file for a divorce. Each day kept coming faster towards my leaving. We only had time to react to the present situation.

I am unsure if Pam and I discussed the situation long enough; we addressed the problem we had and resolved it.

Soon after our decision, Pam and I completed all the paperwork for the credit union. I never looked back at what we did as wrong; I'm not sure what Pam had thought. We did what was needed to do so that Pam could access the checking account. I assigned my life insurance to Pam. After all, should something happen to me, the life insurance the military had on me would allow her to move back home to Massachusetts. The checking account she now can access would help her begin a new life.

The Heart-Wrenching Farewell

She was now twenty-one hundred miles from our home. As for me, this would be my third Christmas outside of the USA since I joined the military.

Aircraft maintenance was nothing more than a constant reel of sacrifices. It meant packing up your life and moving to a new base, receiving orders to deploy overseas, or being sent to remote locations. My career field had always been a relentless test of Pam's patience and devotion throughout our short but meaningful relationship.

When I learned I was going to Thailand, my heart sank like a stone in an endless sea. Pam and I just signed a new lease for a new apartment, carefully selected furniture to fill our space, and made plans for the future.

While living in our old apartment near the university, we visited the humane animal shelter one fateful day and rescued a puppy. The idea of having a puppy had been a dream of mine for quite some time, and I believed it would bring us closer together. As I embarked on another TDY (Temporary Duty) assignment, I thought having a furry companion around would comfort Pam and protect her. Our friends, Duane and Sally, had a dog, and it seemed to be a source of solace for Sally when Duane was away. I imagined Pam feeling the same way, although, in retrospect, it might not have been what she truly desired.

One sunny Saturday morning, as I washed our car in the driveway, I playfully placed James, our neighbor's son whom we were watching, and our puppy, Molly, in a shallow puddle of water. I took my camera out to capture the adorable moment of James splashing around in a dirty puddle with our dog. Pam, however, walked out, her expression a mix of surprise and concern. She asked what I was thinking, and I had no answer. Not angry, she simply inquired if I had put James in the water. As Pam lifted James from the puddle, I was told to get our dog out of the water as well. I lifted the wet and wiggly puppy from the puddle and brought him back inside. *'Really?'* Pam said, raising an eyebrow, and then she instructed me to bathe both James and Molly. I had undoubtedly landed myself in the doghouse.

Heartbreaking Goodbye

After a few weeks with our beloved puppy and the excitement of securing a new apartment, we were blindsided by the news that pets were strictly prohibited in our new living space.

We faced a problematic situation in our new living space. The realization shattered my heart. We faced a difficult choice: either find another apartment we could afford or say goodbye to our cherished puppy. Ultimately, we decided to return Molly to the humane shelter.

On a somber Sunday, shortly after signing the lease for our new apartment, we embarked on a melancholic journey to the humane shelter. I carried our beloved Molly inside as Pam remained in the car, as she was too heartbroken to watch us leave Molly behind. I clutched Molly close to my chest, her warm, trusting eyes reflecting confusion and sadness. With trembling hands, I donated the fee required for the services. I reluctantly placed her into the arms of a caring volunteer. As I turned to leave, I couldn't resist stealing one last glance at her. Her big, expressive eyes locked onto mine, her tail wagging joyfully hanging out, silently asking, *'What's going on?'* With a heavy heart, I turned away and walked out as quickly as I could.

Inside the car, the air was thick with the weight of sorrow. I remained silent, struggling to suppress the emotions that were building in me. I desperately tried to avoid thinking about what I had just done, keeping my mind occupied with anything but the image of Molly. I believed I could handle it until I pulled away from the shelter. Barely a few blocks from the parking lot, my composure crumbled. I broke down completely, realizing I was far from the pillar of strength I thought I was.

I cried uncontrollably, and it must have terrified Pam. She tried valiantly to console me, but the pain ran too deep. I felt an overwhelming guilt for giving that innocent puppy false hope only to return her to the shelter she had come from. It was a tormenting decision that haunted me for a long time.

With Pam's unwavering support, I eventually found a way to cope with losing my loyal four-legged friend.

Sad Farewell to Pam

As we bid farewell to Pam just days after celebrating her birthday on November 27, a heavy sorrow consumed me. That night, we went to Pinnacle Peaks to celebrate. After dinner, we walked the old west towne and stopped at several stores.

The looming departure was weighing heavy on my shoulders. It meant leaving behind the warmth of home and several projects, the prominent being moving Pam from our present apartment to our new apartment near the base. The gravity of this parting became painfully evident.

Pam, steadfast as a rock and supportive of this upcoming mission, drove me to the squadron on the morning of my departure. Her eyes held pride and worry, reflecting the emotions swirling within us. As I gathered my belongings and walked towards the flightline gate, I glanced back at her retreat; I hadn't grasped how this departure driven by duty would sow unease in our relationship.

Walking away from where Pam and I held our last hug and kisses, I passed through the guarded gate onto the flightline. I couldn't shake the feeling that this separation would stretch longer than any previous missions in my Air Force career. Seeing Pam drive off in our recently purchased Novi brought an added ache within me.

As I boarded the aircraft, our DC-130E, which was requested for this particular mission, would be whisking me to another land; questions started to tug at my thoughts throughout the journey across the Pacific, which would take us five days. Since joining the Air Force, this will be my 5th crossing over the Pacific Ocean.

Flying to Thailand, the entire crossing sadness was with me as thoughts of Pam lingered incessantly in my mind.

Linebacker II Ends

The peace negotiations resumed in late January of 1973, and the extra support personnel would be sent home. I was glad to hear that, and since we would be leaving within a week, I wrote a short letter to Pam about my return and the departure date of January 23, 1973. Operation Linebacker II ended.

Six months later, I was awarded the U.S. Air Force Commendation Medal for participating in this operation. I received two service stars for the Vietnam Service Medal. Service stars are awarded for each of the campaigns I was involved with.

USAir Force Commendation Medal Awarded for Linebacker II

It was a bittersweet moment when the award was presented to me, a rush of emotions swelling inside as the ceremony unfolded. As the room buzzed with applause and jubilant chatter, an unmistakable void weighed heavily on my heart- the absence of Pam.

Entangled Hearts

While all the other attendees were fortunate enough to have a loved one by their side to pin the prestigious award onto their service coat, I found myself alone. The absence of Pam was palpable, like a missing piece of a puzzle that would never fit into place.

In the poignant, Sally, my dear friend's wife, stepped forward to graciously do the honors. Her warm smile and comforting presence provided a small measure of solace amid my sorrow. Tears began to flow down my cheeks as she accepted the award to pin on me. Though it couldn't replace the warmth and love that Pam would have brought that moment, I was genuinely grateful for Sally's kind gesture.

In the end, as I glanced at the gleaming award, I couldn't help but think that while the physical symbol was there, what was missing from it was Pam, the person who meant the world to me and who I wished could have been there to share in that unforgettable moment.

US Air Force Vietnam Service Medal w/3 service stars
Each Service star represents a campaign during which
I was involved with.

US Air Force Vietnam Medal

While doing a routine pre-flight inspection on the aircraft that would be sent back to Davis-Monthan, I found corrosion in the centre wing of the support structure of the number 2 dry bay. The dry bay is where the fuel lines and valves direct fuel to the engine, cross over to other engines, or allow fuel into the tanks. I reported this to my flight chief, who verified and reported the corrosion to the maintenance control officer. I entered my findings into the 781A aircraft discrepancy forms. I left the aircraft status symbol open until the day shift supervisor confirmed it.

The following morning shift change, Tech Sergeant Frederick, my night shift supervisor, reported the turnover of the aircraft statuses to Master Sergeant Hinkley, the day shift supervisor. After they had discussed the problems found, Master Sergeant Hinckley went to the aircraft with the corrosion to view it and verify it as a grounding item.

Now that both supervisors had seen the corrosion area, they took their findings to the maintenance officer with their results for a decision. It was determined the severity of the discovery was a grounding item. A follow-up from the maintenance officer was performed when he came out to the aircraft. I was still on the plane when he approached me and asked what I thought of the corrosion and whether it was a grounding item.

Entangled Hearts

He asked to be shown the area, and we both went on top of the wing to the number 2 dry bay and viewed the corrosion. After he saw where the corrosion was located, he returned to his office. He called both supervisors back to his office. He told them that the corrosion was bad enough to send the aircraft back to Lockheed for repair instead of trying to repair it on station. Once I was told the news, I added the red 'X' in the symbol block of the 781A forms.

Once we found the corrosion on the aircraft, the maintenance officer knew that one of the aircraft on the station had to return to D-M; he decided to send back that aircraft with the corrosion, and with it, he authorized the six maintenance crew chiefs who were returning back to D-M as pax with the plane. We were no longer needed, and normal operations were restored. The maintenance officer authorizes a one-time ferry flight on that aircraft. It would be sent to Lockheed once we landed at D-M.

The highest-ranking crew chief to return with the aircraft was an E-4. That was me. I was told I was the most experienced E-4 on the return trip.

I would be the crew chief, and an E-3 of my choice would be my assistant. I was honored to have been selected as the primary crew chief for returning the aircraft to Davis-Monthan. Another crew chief, if needed, would ferry it from D-M to Georgia.

Our trip from Thailand would take five days minimum. Taking a C-130 from Thailand was a long flight and an exhausting journey. Long hours listening to the engine's hum, feeling a prop vibration at times before we get it back in sync, and the fishtailing you could swing with should you be fortunate enough to ride in the far back of the aircraft. It would take its toll on you.

The longest flight would be from Hawaii to Tucson, taking over twelve hours of actual flight time and landing with enough fuel to make one go around if we had to. In other words, we would have left just enough fuel to produce fumes in our main wing tanks and no fuel in our external tanks. There was no margin for error on crossing that last segment of our trip.

Robert A. Crothers

We left U-Tapao at about noon on January 23rd and flew to Clark Air Base in the Philippines. Clark Air Base was the first base I was stationed at right out of maintenance school. At Clark, I spent sixteen months of upgrade training on the C-130 aircraft. Even after my upgrade training, I had more to learn about that aircraft. Shortly after receiving my five-skilled level crew chief, I was selected to attend engine-run school for the C-130. Upon completing engine run school, I flew in and out of Cam Rahn Bay, Vietnam, sometimes as a crew chief and other times as support personnel. The C-130s supported mission runs in and throughout South Vietnam.

Now, three years later, landing at Clark looks different from when I was there from 1969 to June 1970.

They still had several C-130Bs on the base, so I walked over to the hanger after I completed my post-flight inspection for tomorrow's flight. Upon entry into the hangar, I saw 5 or 6 guys I was first stationed with at Clark. We all were surprised to see each other as we had never thought we would reenlist for a second term. Then, a former supervisor from those days at Clark came out of his office and was surprised to see me there. He was one of my reporting officials during my training. He came over, and we talked for a while. When I told him I would be walking over to the billeting, he said there were 3 extra maintenance trucks and to get the keys from his office, take one, and use it as needed. '*Of course, the vehicle was not to be used off base,*' he said. I was glad I made the stop at the hangar.

After getting my billeting for the night, I went to the Airmen's Club for dinner. The club seemed empty; very few E-4s and below were in the main dining room. In the main ballroom, this large plate glass once housed Filipino girls brought in from downtown Angeli City outside the base. The girls were there for us to have them dine with and dance with. That was the way they made their money. A take-off from the dime-a-dance girl in the forties during World War II. The rule was the girls could not go off base with you. But now that room was empty.

Entangled Hearts

When I was stationed there, it was packed every evening. And airmen dancing and a live band playing. Now, there is barely a soul in the place.

The next morning, I arrived at our aircraft early and did my preflight inspection. My assistant called for one fuel truck to pump enough fuel on it to get us to Guam. Then, we opened the ramp to the inflight drop position and raised the cargo door. The first crew member out was the flight engineer. He did his flight-ready inspection, sat on the ramp, and waited for the crew. When the flight engineer saw the crew coming out in two trucks with furniture in the back, he got up. He then walked to Bulkhead 245 and retrieved the slip-stick, weight, and balance book to redo the aircraft weight and balance for this trip.

I thought, where will they place all that furniture and stuff in the name of God? Many of the crew had purchased rattan furniture. Others bought stereo systems to bring back home. I had left the grasshopper arms attached to the ramp, allowing the ramp to be opened in flight for airdrops. This would allow them to back up the trucks to the ramp and unload their purchases. That was it for me; the crew would have to load their purchases within the limited space in the cargo bay with the help of the flight engineer. He would recalculate the weight and balance of the aircraft so the aircraft's centre of gravity would be balanced for flight.

This aircraft was not designed for carrying cargo. It was a drone-carrying aircraft with a unique compartment just aft of the bulkhead 245. There was little space from the back of the drone command module to the cargo ramp. We also had pax (passengers) onboard, so they had to have troop seats accessible. When the crew was done loading, there was no space left except for the few cargo seats. All the purchases had taken up the remaining space of what was once a cargo bay, now loaded with furniture, stereos, and large speakers. Now secured by the flight engineer, we would depart the base after the pilots posted their flight plan with operations. The next stop is the Rock, a.k.a. Guam.

Since none of the drone crew were flying back with us, I was the one, along with my assistant, handling ground operations during the engine starts for our flight. I would put the younger airmen next to me as we performed engine start. The younger airman needed actual experience calling out engine start to be signed off in his 623 OJT records. Once all four engines were running and the crew confirmed the engine gauges were suitable for take-off, I entered through the crew entry door, pulled it up behind me, and proceeded to the flight deck, where I stood between the flight engineer and the pilot.

As we taxied, I saw those remaining C-130s silently sitting in their parking spots. Those ramps that were once filled with C-130Bs now had few. Once, the hustle and bustling wash rack of C-130s are now empty and silent. Once a significant stopping at this base terminal, the tarmac now lays bear with civilian aircraft like the DC-8s and Boeing 707s. Names like Braniff, Pan Am, and United no longer arrive daily. Those were the carriers we would be placed on to ferry us to and from the WORLD. Now, just a lone C-141A was sitting near the base operations on the tarmac that once housed my memories of Clark. It was sad to see this, knowing this base was a mecca of activity at one time.

Soon, our aircraft turned onto the active runway. I sat on the crew bunk and watched our takeoff. The DC-130 is a thing of beauty in my eyes. If you were to have an affair, it was with the love of that airplane. It challenged you, as did a woman; when it flew well, it was like a wife who loved you.

We are now airborne, banking toward the east and on our second leg to go home, Guam. We climbed out to our altitude of about twenty thousand feet and were heavier than usual. That extra load of furniture has given us a little heavy tail, as we had our nose up attitude and tail down. Flying like this was a little unsettling at first and would be for the next sixty minutes of flight hours until we burned off enough fuel from our external tanks.

Entangled Hearts

One of the young maintenance troops returning with us had purchased a hammock and strung it above the cargo ramp. Little did this troop know about C-130 fishtails. Meaning it sways, yaws, side to side. It was comical to see this guy in the back, lying in his hammock, swinging back and forth. Not long after the young maintainer had been in his hammock, he started learning about aircraft fishtailing; he would also learn of the slight heat in the area where he would try to sleep. It gets cold in the rear of the C-130, as the underfloor heat stops at the ramp, and sleep is nearly impossible in the cargo bay area. The second problem with his placement of the hammock was that it was near the location of the urinal and crapper. Lesson learned.

Airplane Maintenance and Preparation

As the sun dipped below the horizon, casting a warm golden glow over Guam, our journey ended. We arrived on this enchanting island in the late afternoon, with the promise of adventure in the air on tomorrow's flight.

Upon touchdown, my assistant and I, fueled by a shared dedication to our mission, embarked on a meticulous inspection of the aircraft's heart – the centre wing. We sought to ensure that this soaring marvel, which had carried us safely to this distant destination, remained free from any structural imperfections or the insidious grip of corrosion.

After each flight, as the engines, we would meticulously scrutinize our faithful companion. In these moments, under the vast Pacific sky, our bond with the plane deepened. We knew that a vigilant watch over its well-being was essential to the safety of our journey.

With our checks complete and the aircraft condition deemed sound, we turned our attention to the tasks that would allow us to soar once more. The fading light of the day saw us carrying out our basic post-flight routines with precision and care, ensuring that every detail was attended to.

The next day brought with it a promise of a new adventure, and to prepare for it, I deliberately chose to fuel the plane the following day. It was a decision made not out of necessity but from a place of prudence and foresight. By tending to our aircraft's needs ahead of time, I spared myself the worry of potential fuel leaks or seepage, granting us the peace of mind to fully embrace the boundless possibilities of the skies.

In those moments, as we readied ourselves for the next journey ahead, I couldn't help but feel a sense of anticipation and excitement uniquely known to those who live their lives in the embrace of the open skies.

The morning of our journey will take us to the intriguing destination of Wake Island, a remote and diminutive landmass in the vast Pacific Ocean expanse.

Our anticipation was fueled by the unique terrain awaiting our take-off from a runway that reportedly ascends as you traverse it, culminating in a sudden drop-off at the end, like a natural cliff. This natural wonder beckoned, and I couldn't wait to witness it.

With our aircraft now at the end of the taxiway and our engine runup completed, the pilot began pushing the throttles to military (also known as takeoff), brakes on, and holding us back. As I looked out the pilot's side window and back toward the engines, I could see the air being cut by our props and going over the wings. You could feel the plane wanting to fly as it jerked forward and bounced. Finally, the pilot released the brakes, and our aircraft started to roll forward; the flight engineer sat forward in his seat and watched the engine gauges intensely as the co-pilot called off our speed. I was standing just behind the pilot, holding onto the back of his headrest as I wanted to look out and down when we crossed the threshold. We were halfway through the twelve-thousand-foot runway when I heard the co-pilot call out the *rotation*. Our nose started to come up, and blue skies were in front. The pilot held the aircraft straight and nose high. I peered out his side window, looking down to see the clefts of Guam, where legion had it; many an aircraft had plummeted over it, including a B-52. We have now slipped the bonds of earth ties; not seeing any aircraft at the bottom of those cliffs, I returned to the crew bunk, where I sat until we arrived at Wake.

Wake Island

After six hours of flying, we approached Wake Island, and you could see the entire island out of the cockpit's windscreen as we flew towards it. The ocean would be in front and behind us as we approached our landing. The runway ran the entire length of the island. Our wheels were now on the ground; we had stopped our aircraft just shy of the beach on the other end of the runway. The pilot made a U-turn on the runway, taxied us back to operations, and parked our aircraft in front of the operation building.

Wake Island is small; I can see everything from our cockpit window. People live on this island. It had limited lodging for us. The crew and the other maintenance personnel left the aircraft. The first assistant crew chief and I stayed and ready the plane for tomorrow's flight. As we cleaned the aircraft from today's flight, I noticed several in-flight meal boxes were not opened. I opened one as I gathered them up and went to find my assistant. In it was fried chicken. It is one of the better in-flight meals you could get. The other had a roast beef sandwich. That was given to my assistant. With our meals, we sat outside on the ramp in front of the nose. We enjoyed a wonderful evening meal on a beautiful tropical island in the Pacific.

That evening, my assistant and I spent the night onboard the aircraft in the two crew bunks on the flight deck. My assistant slept on the upper bunk, and I took the lower. It was a warm evening with a gentle breeze coming from the water. We removed the upper hatch above the top crew bunk and opened the two side windows in the cockpit, where a warm but gentle breeze made our rest pleasant. It was a perfect evening spent on the aircraft. The only person lacking from this experience was Pam. Imagine having Pam all to myself on this tropical Island. I could picture it now! I needed to stop that daydreaming as it brought those thoughts to tears.

The next morning, my assistant and I would use the ops (operations) bathroom to clean up. I also requested a fuel truck to be sent out to the aircraft.

The flight engineer was the first aircrew member to arrive and do his acceptance walk-around. He walked back to base operations, meeting with the other crew members. My assistant and I stayed and readied the plane as the other maintenance personnel went to base operations for breakfast and to bring out our in-flight meals.

The in-flight meals were what I thought were good. It's not as good as a hot meal at the chow hall, but it's better than having nothing. And the box lunches we got from Wake were one of the best. The in-flight kitchen spared nothing on these meals. We got more than usual. Each box had a roast beef sandwich, one leg and one breast of cold fried chicken, two cupcakes, an apple, an orange drink, and a bag of potato chips. This would hold us until we reached Midway Island. Another long and tedious flight crossing the pond.

On to Midway

As we left Wake and headed Northeast towards Midway, our aircraft flew better than ever. We did not encounter significant malfunctions that could not be fixed, as if the aircraft knew it had to make it home again. It was smooth flying all the way into Midway.

As we approached the island of Midway, the tower radioed us and told us that we had to make a fly-by as gooney birds had come in and landed on the runway, claiming it as theirs. The gooney birds had just gotten in for the mating season.

As we came in for a landing, we were treated to a real-life avian vaudeville act! Picture this: Our aircraft approaches the runway, and there's this 'Operations Truck' doing its best NASCAR impression, chasing after the runway-invading birds like they're feathered fugitives. They're just loitering on the runway, giving us the avian version of 'No Vacancy.' After what felt like an eternity (okay, maybe just 15 minutes), the tower reluctantly gave us the green light. So, we descended like a top-gun pilot, touched down smoother than a baby's bottom, and our pilots pulled throttles into 'full reverse,' and the props pushed the air forward as fast as they could. We are braking so hard you think we're trying to win a drag race.

But here's the kicker: just as we taxi towards the hanger, those 'gooney' birds, clearly harboring resentment for being removed just for us to land, once again occupied the runway. Their ambitions decide it's a great time to stage a comeback!

As the crew and those flying as pax exited the aircraft and walked to the hangar, the gooney birds followed them to their lodging.

Entangled Hearts

Not being afraid of us, the birds continued to walk right beside those going to their accommodation. As they did, the birds began peaking at the luggage they carried. Laughing as I watched the crew trying to dodge them as best they could was funny. And shoving them away was fruitless. These birds had no fear of any humans as they ruled the island.

My assistant and I did a postflight and closed the aircraft. We used tie-down straps to secure the two paratroop doors near the ramp. And placed a lock specially made for the crew door. This would discourage any squib (a term used for navy sailors) from gaining entrance and stealing parts or those items in the back. Since we were a different-looking aircraft, most wanted to see what we had inside and why we had pods under our wings. Also, all the rattan furniture and stereos some of the guys were bringing home are loosely tied to the floor. Having a couple of those Navy guys in our aircraft, all the stereos would be gone in minutes.

With the aircraft now secured, my assistant and I walked to the hanger that housed our quarters. The pathway to the hanger was full of gooney birds. You could not walk without tripping over one, two, or more gooney birds as they were not afraid of humans and were all over the path. They would not move at all for us when we approached them. They owned the island, and we were just in their way. Some gooney birds walked with us to the hangar. Nothing but gooney birds everywhere.

I got up early the next morning and went directly to our aircraft. Again, I checked the wing root corrosion to see if any changes had occurred during our flight. Nothing had changed. I saw my assistant walking out from the top of the aircraft wing. I yelled at him and asked if he had called for a fuel truck, and he responded. This young airman is becoming a fine crew chief.

The flight crew had filed its flight plan to Hickam and brought out our flight lunches. Since this would only be about a five-hour flight, some passed on the flight lunch.

We had spent twelve hours on Midway as Midway was run by the Navy. Many rumors about how they treated the Air Force with their antics were known by most. We did not experience any such antics for that one night.

Again, we were held up by the gooney birds on the active runway. And again, the ops officer had to go out with his truck and run the birds off the runway so we could get to Hawaii and be closer to home.

Birds were now clear of the runway. We made our lineup for takeoff. And as we rolled down the runway, those birds headed right back onto the runway. With our aircraft nose now coming up, we managed to make our take-off without incident of hitting a gooney bird, and we were up and heading to Hawaii. Our flight time to Hawaii was just a mere four hours.

Hawaii Bound

After a few hours of flight, I saw the Island of Oahu from the pilot's front windscreen. What most people call a windshield is a windscreen on an airplane.

As we journeyed to Oahu, we were provided custom forms to complete. During the flight, the engineer left his seat to spray the aircraft interior about an hour out from landing in Hawaii. I filled his seat while he sprayed this DDT in the cargo bay. This procedure was a requirement by the government of Hawaii when returning from Asia. The Hawaiian government did not want any intrusive insects coming into their island. But somehow, those insects manage to get in!

I was asked to assist in handing out the required customs forms to every member on board. For some pax (passengers), it was their first trip out of the country, and they never filed a customs form; I helped them with it. Customs would collect the completed forms upon our arrival at Hickam, as they would meet us on the tarmac. We had to declare all purchases from the Philippines and the amount of money we were bringing back into the United States. We were allowed so many purchases duty-free. Luckily, we were military, and the government made sure we didn't have much income!

As we descended into Hickam, I stood and looked out the pilot side window. I deeply appreciated the incredible opportunities the Air Force offered me to both work on aircraft and soar alongside them. My role as a crew chief was incredibly fulfilling, granting me numerous advantages during flights, including the privilege of being on the flight deck.

I could see ships below us as we crossed over them, just waiting to pull into port at Pearl Harbour. We circled the island and made our landing from the east. We land on Oahu using the same runway as the commercial airlines. Then, instead of taxing to the commercial airport, we turned off the active runway and taxied to the awaiting transient alert truck that would guide us to the area where Customs would be waiting.

As the pilot followed the transit truck to Hickam and our parking spot, I walked to the aircraft's rear and lowered the cargo ramp to the in-flight drop position. Once parked, Customs boarded the plane and collected the forms we filled out before landing. Next, they did a quick drug inspection with their dogs, and afterward, I was asked to close the plane ramp, paratroop doors, and all escape hatches and exits. I was the last one out and closed the crew entry door, where the customs officer sealed it for the next twenty-four hours. Agriculture rules for all aircraft, military or civilian, arriving from Asia had to rest twenty-four hours in case of insects on board. I couldn't figure out why they were not concerned about insects hiding away in places like the wheel wells but also the stowaway snakes. Those Asian snakes would cross the ramp and into and onto the aircraft, mainly during the night when the temperature was lower. You could find snakes in two places: the nose wheel well, a favorite spot for them, and the engine fire bottles just above the left main landing gear wheel well. There's nothing like coming face to face with a Bore Constrictor peering at you.

After closing the aircraft, my assistant and I called for the base taxi to take us to Billet, where we were assigned rooms. Being an enlisted non-flight crew member, my lodging was not air-conditioned, as were those on flight status. I was given a room and went to it with my overnight luggage. The room was warm, and I opened the large jalousie glass windows to let some of the breeze into the room.

A city bus was allowed on base to pick up those who wanted to go downtown. You did not need a car in Hawaii as the buses will take you to any part of the island you wanted to see.

It may have taken twenty minutes to get to the beach part of the island, but we were now in Waikiki. We traveled through a run-down part of Oahu, which was pretty shanty. Construction was everywhere we went. The tourist section of town was going through a growth period, with lots of new construction. Every sidewalk we walked on was under scaffolding.

I left my group and decided to walk on the beach alone. Thoughts of Pam and how we walked the beaches back home when we were just dating as teenagers fill my mind. Walking through the Royal Hawaiian Hotel, my thoughts of Pam became more vivid. That is when I thought of bringing her and visiting Hawaii. Being military, we could go to base operations at D-M and sign up for a standby flight with either a tanker or cargo aircraft heading to Hawaii. I thought she might like that, riding stand-by on a military aircraft. No luxury seating; she would have to endure those canvas seats just like us. But she could get to the flight deck and see the flight controls and all the gauges it takes to watch the aircraft operations. There was no cost to us unless we could not get a flight back to D-M. She would like Hawaii for a visit, not for us to be stationed there for three years. I would not even want to be stationed here for three years myself. Visit yes!

After spending my day downtown Waikiki, I was exhausted from the heat and all the walking I had done. The sun was setting, and I wanted to return to base to eat before the chow hall closed. I caught the bus that took me back to the base, which was full of other military personnel.

My first night at Hickam was warm and muggy. While I lay in bed, thinking of Pam, sweat rolled down my forehead and out of my arms and legs. Off in the distance, I heard ukulele music. I was awake most of that night because of the humidity in my room. It was so bad that my sheets were wet from sweat. I had to take several showers that evening just to get a few hours of sleep.

The next morning, another free day to explore the island. The bus cost was a quarter; you could get transfer passes to change buses to other parts of the island.

There was absolutely nothing going on at the beach that day. My assistant crew chief went to explore independently. I remained at the beach, sat on the sand, watched the waves and surfers, and thought of Pam being with me. There was little difference between being at the beach in Hawaii and Massachusetts except for the warm water and the lack of sand dunes. Well, maybe more than I thought!

With thoughts of Pam, as I sat on the beach, I began to think how she might enjoy the warm tropical breezes, the hotel's pristine beaches, and the warm ocean water. Of course, knowing Pam, I knew that none of these beaches would compare to our shores back home in Massachusetts.

My assistant crew chief and I met up near where we parted and walked the main road, and as we did, we found a few bars along the way and stopped to see what they were like. They were just bars, nothing spectacular.

That evening, a message on my billeting door read I needed to meet Customs at the aircraft at twelve hundred hours tomorrow and have them unlock the crew door. It also said that we were scheduled for takeoff at twenty hundred hours. With that, I retired for the evening.

Customs didn't come out as scheduled. It was well after thirteen hundred hours when they finally did show. Once they released the plane to me, I opened the aircraft up to get it cool inside. I opened every window in the flight deck and the top hatch. Then, I removed the escape hatch windows in the cargo bay, opened the two paratroop doors, positioned the cargo ramp down, and raised the cargo door.

Entangled Hearts

As my assistant and I began to inspect the plane, I had him call for a fuel truck. After closing all those doors I had opened, we serviced all main fuel tanks in the wings and the two external tanks to their fullest for this final leg of the trip home. As I began filling the tanks from the SPR panel (single point refuel panel), I hoped there would be no issues with those fuel shutoff valves. Had there been any, I would have serviced the fuel from the top of the wing as there were wing refuel ports for each main tank, and the external tanks had one. The load will be maximum. Then, during the remainder of the hot afternoon, I prayed we would not get a fuel leak or any fuel seeping out the rivets on the bottom of the wings. I took a vigil watch for any fuel seep or drip! But I had my fuel stop stick that I could apply to a seep that would hold a fuel seep short term.

Each pound of JP-4 pumped into the wing's main cells and external fuel cell (tank) would add weight to the main struts as JP-4 weighs 6.7 lbs. per gallon. In calculating our take-off, we use the weight of the fuel, not the number of gallons. I could hear the main struts groaning as if to say really, you need that much fuel? More moans and groans were heard as the landing struts lowered under the weight of the fuel.

An aircraft has weight limits for take-offs, and the temperature and humidity play a part in calculating the required length of runway needed to lift off.

Now fully loaded with fuel, I would watch the underside of the wings all afternoon for any fuel leaks or seepage. The fuel vapors in our dry bays will increase. I went to the topside to open all inspection panels to allow them to vent the fumes out. With that hot sun beating down on the plane, the aircraft's skin was hot to the touch, and I had to wear gloves to keep our hands from burning when touching the aircraft's skin.

Now that we had added fuel and weight to the aircraft, my assistant and I would begin servicing all hydraulic reservoirs and then ask transient alert to bring out a B-1 or B-5 stand to service the engines with oil and check the prop fluid. After servicing all engines, the 781K had shown that S.O.A.P. samples were to be pulled. We do this every twenty-five flight hours. I could have easily done the S.O.A.P. (spectrum oil analysis program) samples but added a note to the 781 A that S.O.A.P. would be taken at D-M upon completion of this flight. That meant they would have been twelve hours overdue. An S.O.A.P. is looking for the metal in the oil, indicating an engine problem.

After we had finished with the engines, I requested a high-pressure air cart, MA-1, be brought out to allow us to service the struts to the correct height under our current fuel load. Struts are the aircraft's shock absorbers and are necessary items to be serviced with different aircraft weights. Most of the time, we did not have to adjust them as the aircraft weight rarely changed at the home station. But on this final leg of our trip, we exceeded what was normal for us with the present load on the struts. If not done correctly, you could have one higher than the other when you land. I have seen aircraft land with one high wing and lopsided as they taxied back to a parking spot. Someone not well-trained in strut servicing would find it the scariest job. Struts move up or down quickly when being serviced. You increase the pressure when you think there's not enough high-pressure air in the strut to move them up. They can really take off like a jackrabbit if you are not careful. Catching you off guard before you can shut off high-pressure airflow. Quickly putting a new tech and even some season techs in panic mode.

Strut Surprises: A Crew Chief's Training Tale

During my career, I've observed new crew chiefs attempting to qualify using the MA-1 air cart and servicing struts to manage different aircraft loads. While it is possible to do this task solo, having a team of two is optimal: one operating the MA-1 to regulate hose pressure and the other managing the Shrader valve on the strut. These struts can be unexpectedly noisy, startling you as they ascend or descend. Occasionally, they move swiftly, adding to the surprise factor.

Women were now entering the career field of AFSC 43151F. I was assigned to train a new crew chief on servicing main struts during a training session months earlier. I placed the trainee in the left wheel well. Putting her on the left main forward tire, I positioned myself behind it just forward of the aft tire while I stood on the boogey strut. Instructing her on the procedure from our tech manual.

I had her remove the yellow safety cap and place it in her pants pocket, then cut and remove the steel safety wire, ensuring she did not create fod (foreign object damage). Securing her adjustable wrench on the jam nut, just lower than the stem, she slowly opened the jam nut to the Shrader valve until it was finger loose, then turned it by hand until it stopped. She then placed her crescent wrench on the nut that controls the valve opening. Then, I yelled out to the operator who would control the MA-1 line pressure. She sat and waited to see if the strut would move, and when it didn't, she asked if she should open the jam nut more? Just as she slowly opened the valve to allow more high-pressure air, the strut started to move up. It moved up slowly at first, making popping sounds and jumps. She asked if she should open it more, and I said to give it a quarter turn. That's when the strut took off and rose to full length.

She was taken off guard by the speed of the strut rising; she jumped off the tire and out of the wheel well towards the MA-1 cart. She made it out without hitting her head on the wheel well door as she exited. The operator of the MA-1 shut down the pressure line to the strut when he saw her come out. I climbed up on the wheel and closed the valve off. Now, we had to reverse the process and lower the strut.

Many trainees have run out of the main wheel well when learning how to service aircraft struts. When they did, if they were learning to lower the strut and left the Shrader valve open, they soon realized that all the hydraulic fluid squirted into the wheel well and oozed down the strut and all over the tire and brake. This caused a major clean-up for that new trainee! It would also cause the aircraft to be jacked and the strut to be serviced appropriately.

It is a bit scary when the strut you are servicing decides to move up rapidly or down suddenly. As a trainee myself, I was caught off guard the first time. I froze, kneeling atop the main tire, watching the hydraulic fluid streaming out the top of the Shrader valve as if it were old faithful and all over inside the wheel well. Not to mention hydraulic fluid dripping all over my face and uniform. I was just looking at the valve. Numb to the ears, I did not hear my trainer yelling at me to close the valve. My trainer found his way up next to me and had to take over.

But like all those trained in strut servicing, she too would learn that the strut would not come flying off when it was being serviced with air. Nor would it not be serviceable if it were to bottom out.

As you reverse the process of lowering a strut, you will remove some air from the strut, hoping that you do not bottom out or, worse yet, have hydraulic fluid squirt out the valve. While you continue to release the air from the strut, you may have to add a person on top of the wing or have someone transfer fuel from one wing to the side you are trying to lower the strut on. Placing a couple of people on the wing and bouncing on the side of the landing gear you are trying to lower worked best.

Continue: 'Hawaii Bound'

All maintenance is complete; my assistant and I walk to base ops and the snack bar for a sandwich while we await the flight engineer.

The flight engineer arrived just around 1830 hours to do his preflight. But before he did, he took the aircraft slip-stick out (it was known as a calculator). He recalculated our weight, balance, and roll distance for this evening's takeoff... Then, after his preflight, he and the pilot conferred and agreed on the new aircraft weight and balance for this evening's flight. The pilot called all of us to the nose of the aircraft and gave us our briefing. Nothing was different in the briefing except that this leg of our flight would be the longest, and it was through the night we would fly.

At 1930 hours, we prepared for the engine start. I took the position of ground. After all four engines were running, the flight engineer and pilot conferred with the gauges on each engine that they were all good. Then, they told me to get on board. I raced to the crew entry door, grabbed the attached rope, pulled it up behind me as I entered the aircraft, and secured the door for the flight. Then, I ran up the flight deck stairs to the crew bunk and sat next to my assistant crew chief for our final take-off of this trip.

With limited troop seats in the cargo bay, those not sitting in the drone compartment ended up on the red troop seats; it was first come, first served. Those who arrived early for the flight sat in the drone compartment on the chairs, much more comfortable but unable to lie down. The red troop seats at the aircraft's rear may be uncomfortable, but you can stretch out and sleep.

Also, the warm air pumped into the room made it immensely more comfortable for those sitting there than those riding in the cargo bay behind it.

A few of those traveling back had purchased pool floats. They blew them up and laid them on the troop seats and any space on the floor they could find. Here, they slept during our night trip. The C-130 props can hum you to sleep when riding in the cargo bay. The cargo bay's white dome lights were switched to red. This allowed enough light to find our way back to the urinal. No one would use the honey bucket as if you were the first; you would be tasked to clean it after we landed. And there was no privacy if you used the honey bucket as there was just a curtain to pull around it. On the C-130, you had to rough it if you had to use the commode.

Vivid Hawaiian Sunset Departure

As we embarked from the tropical paradise of Hawaii, our departure was a vibrant dance with the elements. The aircraft poised on the runway like a surfer awaiting the perfect wave, eager to ride the skies. Like a conductor in an orchestra, the tower held us back momentarily, letting us savor the last moments of the island's warmth before granting us permission to soar.

With anticipation humming in the air, we navigated the runway's centre line, the engines purring as if eager to embrace the sky's vast expanse. The runway beneath us stretched like a canvas, guiding our journey to the horizon. As we accelerated, the runway's end seemed elusive, teasing us with the thrill of an extended takeoff.

In the distance, the sun began its descent, casting its golden hues across the sky, painting it with a palette that defied words. Shades of orange, pink, and purple melded together, creating a breathtaking tapestry against the backdrop of the Pacific. The horizon blurred the line between sea and sky, inviting us to join this celestial canvas.

The aircraft's nose lifted gracefully as if bowing to the splendor ahead. Our hearts leapt in unison with the ascending altitude. For a suspended moment, we felt like time itself had paused to admire the spectacle. The beauty of the setting sun accompanied us, a loyal companion bidding us farewell from the west as we turned our flight towards the new coordinates in the east.

With the radiant colors still vivid in our memory, we embarked on the final leg of our journey home and to Pam. Carrying with us the brilliance of that Hawaiian departure, a moment etched in our minds forever.

Sunset Symphony

Honoring the Trans-Pacific Journey and Unwavering Teamwork

With headsets on and as we settled in for the final leg of this extraordinary trip, I could hear the crew talk about the monumental achievement of crossing the vast expanse of the Pacific. This journey wasn't just a routine flight; it was a testament to the resilience and expertise of our exceptional flight crew and the dedicated individuals who maintained our aircraft's airworthiness.

The pilot, co-pilot, flight engineer, and navigator are maestros in their own right. Our passage across the ocean was made with precision and grace. The seamless coordination, unwavering focus, and unyielding commitment to safety guided us through every mile of the journey.

But behind the scenes, the unsung heroes, my assistant crew chief, also deserve accolades. His tireless dedication ensured that the aircraft was airworthy despite its prior bout with corrosion and performed admirably throughout the voyage. His meticulous attention to detail in maintenance held the highest standards, instilling confidence in all who flew on with it.

With each stop along the way, our flight crew and support personnel's camaraderie, professionalism, and dedication have made a daunting expedition into an inspiring tale of triumph over the possibility of adversity.

Once we established our climb to altitude, the flight engineer increased the heat, and warm air started coming out of the vents of the flight deck and cargo bay. Soon, the cargo bay underfloor heating was on, helping those lying on the floor on their float mattresses stay warm.

The air temperature outside the aircraft was at a negative degree, and the underfloor heat had a difficult time keeping up with warmth, but it was enough to prevent frost.

It is now my turn to sleep for a while. I crawled up on the top crew bunk and fell asleep with nothing but pleasant dreams of seeing Pam.

Flight Crew Swap Adventure

Along the way, solace took place with all of us. But we all shared a memorable and unique experience during our flight, with an unexpected turn of events where the aircraft's crew allowed maintenance personnel to take control one person at a time, but never jeopardizing flight safety.

Our flight took an unexpected twist, and it turned out to be one of the most unforgettable moments of our journey. As I drifted off to sleep, I was suddenly roused from my slumber by the gentle swaying and bobbing of the aircraft. It had been moving in a rhythmic pattern of up and down as if it had a mind of its own.

Bleary-eyed, I cracked one eye and peered towards the flight deck. To my astonishment, I saw one of our younger troops at the controls, confidently steering the plane from the co-pilot seat. The crew had decided to let maintenance personnel take a crack at flying the aircraft they maintain.

Before I knew it, we were all getting in on the action, taking turns in various crew positions except the left seat. That seat was always maintained by a pilot. So, I took the right seat, co-piloting the aircraft and having an experience I could never have anticipated. For forty-five exhilarating minutes, I had the thrill of being in control, the wind whistling past the windows as I guided the plane through the night skies.

But the adventure didn't stop there. I later moved to the flight engineer's position, where I became the guardian of the aircraft's vital systems. Monitoring fuel levels, engine requirements, pressurization, and ensuring the wings remained perfectly balanced as we consumed fuel was a bit like reliving the moments when we ran engines on the ground.

I settled into the role and savored every moment, soaking in the unique sensation of being so intimately connected to the plane's operation.

Incredible as this flight was, it couldn't quite compare to the exhilaration of certain other life experiences, like the first time I shared an intimate connection with Pam. That's a story for another time, but I'll always remember this flight as a close second in the ranks of unforgettable moments.

As we pressed on to the east, the sun began its ascent on the horizon ahead. Our DC-130 inched its way toward Los Angeles, California. Speed was a luxury we couldn't afford in this aircraft. The view before us was nothing short of breathtaking, much like Pam.

The pilot changed our heading for Davis-Monthan once we were over land. There are just a few more hours to go.

Excited to Return to D-M

As our plane soared over the Rincon Mountains into Tucson, the morning sun burst through our windscreen with hues of gold and pink, having the crew place their sun visors down to shade their eyes for this landing. With the sun casting a gentle glow over the mountains and to the awaking city below, the streets lay in a serene quietude, as if holding their breath in anticipation of the bustling day ahead. From above, the cityscape slowly came to life, with faint murmurs of activity starting to stir among the buildings.

Amidst this tranquil awakening, D-M appeared on the horizon. The flight crew, efficient and composed, guided the aircraft in a graceful descent towards the base. Through the windows, I eagerly drank in the view, a mixture of exhilaration and impatience bubbling within me. I longed to reunite with Pam, the early hour doing nothing to diminish the eagerness coursing through my veins.

Pam, no doubt, was already up and about, preparing for my arrival at the squadron; I envision her bustling with energy, ready to welcome as the city gradually transitioned from the tranquility of dawn to the vivaciousness of a new day. The anticipation of our reunion heightens with every passing moment, making the final approach to D-M feel like an eternity despite the breathtaking scenery unfurling below.

After we touched down, I hastily made my way from the crew bunk to the side window just behind the pilot. I watch in anticipation as we taxied back to our section of the flightline. My eyes caught the sight of the expeditor truck parked off to our port side, and I knew my friend Duane would be there to guide us into the parking spot. I was eager to disembark. When we parked and the engines were shut down,

Duane ascended the crew stairs, and our warm greetings filled the air. He inquired about the flight and any necessary repairs for the plane. I was happy to report that everything had gone smoothly, and there were no significant issues other than the root wing corrosion. I also mentioned that I had meticulously serviced the aircraft hydraulics and engines before we departed from Hickam and that S.O.A.P. samples needed to be pulled and sent to the lab.

With the crew heading off for debriefing and Duane's' team beginning their inspections, those who had purchased items started to unload them to their POVs (personal owners' vehicles). I, however, had no furniture or stereo equipment to deal with, so I exited the plane through the crew entry door, clutching only my bag. I made my way to the crew chief building and out the gate, eager to reunite with Pam, who had not yet arrived. I waited outside the flightline gate, my heart pounding in anticipation. Homecoming was a joyous occasion, but it was made even sweeter by the prospect of seeing Pam again.

As I was leaving the building, Senior Master Sergeant Williams stopped me in my tracks. He delivered the fantastic news that I had the liberty to take a week off to attend to personal matters before I had to return to work. A whole week with Pam felt like a week in paradise!

Second TDY

A familiar notification was received not even three months after my last TDY, signaling the return to Thailand. This time, I would be there for a set number of days.

My regular rotation would have occurred nine months after my signing into the unit. That would have brought my TDY out to August. But I have proven my abilities as a crew chief; I was sent back earlier to replace another crew chief returning from their eighty-nine-day TDY.

An Air Force shortage was in our career field. Staffing experience crew chiefs in our AFSC has hit an all-time low. Most of those in this career field have now been released from their enlistment because of the downsizing of Vietnam. But efforts to bring home our POWs and MIAs were ongoing. Our operations out of Thailand would not end until August 1975. Our unit was experiencing a shortage of qualified crew chiefs. We were sent new graduates from maintenance school. It's an undertaking as we continue juggling two overseas locations under SAC (Strategic Air Command). We are the only turboprop aircraft in a group composed of bombers and tankers. Something we at D-M could feel proud of. Our motto was with P.R.I.D.E. or Professional Results in Daily Efforts. Our personnel supported our aircraft, DC-130A, in Osan, Korea, and our DC-130Es in U-Tapao, Thailand.

As I prepared to leave, I couldn't help shake the ache in my heart, knowing how much Pam may be weathering in my absence. Now that she has experienced the first deployment of me leaving, I hope the second will be easier for her. I thought I knew how difficult it would be with me going. We have been in this new apartment only a few months and have made friends with Duane and Sally, another couple from the

Northeast area, Utica, New York; they would be the closest of all friends we have at this time. In this unfamiliar town, where we had yet to build a network of connections, Pam faced the daunting prospect of being far from home without the close support of family, leaving only the hope that this deployment would be more manageable for her.

Pam knew that someone from the squadron would always be her sponsor during any of my deployments should she need help. That person would be the one she could call if help was needed. But unbeknownst to me, she may have already had her support. TSgt. Hinke was from the squadron and was assigned to be her aide while I was deployed.

I'll need money sent to me during this deployment. Since part of our income involves separation pay. While on TDY status and receiving separations, I'm responsible for paying for all meals I eat at the chow hall while deployed. I will take enough money to get me by for the first month.

I left Davis-Monthan for U-Tapao, Thailand, on April 13th, 1972. Pam drove me to the Base Recreation Centre, where I had to report. I'm flying as a pax on an Air Force KC-135A tanker. This time, Pam and I had a short goodbye. Usually, it is a sign of someone's experience in Air Force departures. It made me feel she was used to my departures, but only being my second one; maybe I should have been more concerned? I only wished she had known more of the other squadron wives and girlfriends.

The tanker I would be traveling on was in its U-Tapao rotation. As we are, the tankers are part of SAC and have their rotation schedules. Except that when they ferry an aircraft over, they change crews along the way. The pax just enjoy the travel as they will continue with the plane as flight crews change out.

Once inside the recreation building, we gathered in the area and waited for the base transportation bus to take us to our waiting aircraft.

There are about fifty of us headed to U-Tapao on this rotation. We board the plane and see it is carrying cargo down the middle of the cargo bay, leaving just enough room for us to walk between it and the troop seats. The pilot gave his briefing and estimated when we would arrive at our first stop and RON (rest overnight).

After all the engines were started, the boomer, the crew member who operates the in-flight refueling operations on this aircraft, climbed up into the flight deck. With everything now secured, the tanker taxi to the runway, an emotion of sadness came over me. This was the first time that I had ever felt like this. For most of my career, I never had anyone I had feelings for, so going to TDY was an everyday event. I was that guy that would cheer those who just left a love. But this time was different. I have someone in my life that I care for.

The aircraft sits at the runway's end, and the crew performs their run-up checklist. Ensuring that those engines will perform flawlessly for this flight. Once complete, the pilot pushes, and the co-pilot backs up the pilot, moving all four throttles forward. With his left on the steering control, the pilot keeps this aircraft on the centre line as it travels down the runway. The engine noise increases, and the tanker starts to move down the runway. As it does, the speed increases.

As the aircraft reaches speed, the control of the aircraft transfers from the steering wheel to the rudder pedals. The pilot, keeping our plane on the centre line, now steers the aircraft with the control of the rudder pedals. His left hand now moves to the yoke. His alignment on the centre line is near perfect.

The co-pilot monitors the EPR gauges (engine pressure ratio) and watches as they climb up in numbers until they reach the rotation stage. Then he calls for the pilot *'rotation,'* and the aircraft nose rises and leaves the ground. But this take-off seems unusually long.

Entangled Hearts

Our aircraft continues its roll down the runway. From my red troop seat, I could view our take-off roll from the small portal I sat next to.

As the aircraft continued down the runway, everything seemed normal until I saw our Phase Hanger. This hanger is almost a few thousand feet from the runway overrun.

I heard the water ejectors kick in earlier. (water ejectors provide water into the engine for increased thrust during take-off.)I noticed we were nearing the end, and still, our nose was not coming up. I thought, shouldn't we be in the air by now? Our DC-130 would have been up and flying six thousand feet earlier. Then, we went past the maintenance hangar for our DC-130s. Some maintenance personnel are standing outside the hangar doors, watching us go by. Some even waved at us. Why are you waving? Is it that bad? Now, I am apprehensive as I know the runway's end is coming up and coming up fast! And at the end of this runway, even though it is flat, there is nothing but Cacti for miles. Just as I turned back in my seat, I checked my seat belt and pulled it taunt. Then I take both hands and grab the webbing on either side of me on the seat for added measures. Why, I don't know? Should we run off the runway, it may keep me from being thrown all over. I close my eyes to prepare for a crash. And as I did, I felt the nose began to come up. No Pam was in my thoughts during these few moments of terror!

Low to the ground, we crossed the end of the threshold; I could have picked the blooming flowers off the cactus as we went over them so low. We were climbing. In the few years I have been a crew chief and riding aircraft, C-130s, I have never experienced such a long take-off roll and using up almost twelve thousand feet of the runway.

I am happy that we made it off the ground, and the air is beneath the wings and the top of the wings to pull us upward. I look towards the cockpit and see the crew elated as if this was a normal take-off. Sure glad I didn't have to use my life insurance.

The tanker has no air conditioning; it mixes outside air with the engine heat to condition the air. A large water separator ensures it will not rain inside the cargo bay. The co-pilot turns on the airflow for outside air to cool the interior. He also makes adjustments to the air temperature. Cool air is flowing through the cargo bay now. It was time to settle in for a short ride to March Air Force Base, where we would spend the night.

Peanut Butter

While TDY, SSgt Vogel received a care package, a tradition filled with anticipation for us overseas. These packages, sent by the wives, contained a trove of home comforts: homemade treats, essential clothing, and toiletries. One evening, Vogel, generous as ever, brought his care package to share its delights. Nestled within was an assortment of his wife's cookies, accompanied by a note insisting they were meant for all of us.

The box of cookies found its place on the truck crew seat, a tempting invitation to indulge. Curiosity piqued, I inquired about the unfamiliar cookie called 'snickerdoodles.' My peanut allergy made me cautious, but assurances came that they were devoid of peanuts or peanut butter. Unconvinced, I took a bite, only to recognize the unmistakable taste of peanut butter. Panic set in as I tried to rid my mouth of it, resorting to water and Coke from a nearby snack bar.

Despite my efforts, the lingering taste signals trouble. Within moments, my mouth reacted, a sure sign of the allergen's presence.

When all this took place, it was a shift change. Billy drove to the hooch to get the first shift guys and bring them back to relieve us. But the peanut butter had advanced while he was gone, making me ill.

When we returned to the hooch, I decided to try to remove that peanut butter taste from my mouth one last time. I told my group that I was going to the snack bar, and they also wanted something from there. They gave me their request and the money to purchase their food.

When I arrived at the snack bar, I went to the fountain for drinks and poured myself a Coke. I'm hoping that will do the final wash-out of the peanut butter. It did not work; when they took my hamburger off the grill and added all the condiments they could, I did not wait for it to be wrapped and asked them to give it to me. I knew it was too late as I could feel a change in my face and tongue; they began to swell. It might have been my last meal if the good lord were not watching over me. He must have known I did not carry an EpiPen. The rest of the burgers were put in a sack for me to bring back.

I managed to walk out of the snack bar on my own with the food I was to bring back to the hooch. But while walking back, a severe reaction started to take place in my throat from what peanut butter was in my system. There was nothing that I could do except drop to the cement sidewalk. My eyes were now closed, and my tongue started to swell. I was partially conscious while on the ground and about halfway to my hooch. It just so happened that someone was walking to the snack bar when this happened, and he saw me as I dropped onto the sidewalk. He then noticed I was not moving, and I heard him yell to someone nearby to call the base hospital for an ambulance. This was before 911 and EMTs. He knelt next to me to see what he could do if anything. There was nothing!

Shortly after the call to the hospital, I could hear an ambulance. I was unable to open both eyes at this time. Still on the ground, I managed to get one eye open just enough to see around me. In the haze, through my open eye, I saw several people standing around and watching as the medics tried to get me to respond. I heard that one guy who found me tell the medic that he had just seen me fall to the ground. One of the medics asked me a question, and as I started to answer it, he saw my tongue was swollen. They quickly placed me on a stretcher and brought me to the base hospital.

I arrived at the hospital, was taken into the emergency room, and transferred from the stretcher to a hospital gurney.

I lay on a gurney, a sheet being placed over me, leaving just my face visible. Am I dead? The ER doctor came in and stood over me; a light above me was turned on. It is shining through my closed eyelids. The doctor kept repeating himself by asking me what type of drugs I had taken. I repeated several times that I took no medications or drugs. With my tongue swelling more, I could mumble, '*I was allergic to peanut butter in a cookie I ate.*' He continues to ask about drugs.

There was a shift change in the ER, and another doctor asked what I was in for. The off-duty doctor tells him that I claim I am not on drugs. '*Then what is he claiming?*' the oncoming doctor asked. With a sarcastic voice from the off-duty doctor, he said, '*Peanut butter.*' I could hear the oncoming doctor tell the off-duty doctor he had just attended a conference about peanut allergies. Once the doctor listened to that, he knew what treatment had to be given, and when I heard him tell the nurse to administer a shot of the serum, I relaxed so much I passed out.

Several hours later, I found myself in the hospital ward with needles coming out of my arms. When the nurse saw me awake, she asked me if I needed anything, and I recalled saying no. I asked her what time it was, and she told me, and then she said I had been asleep for twenty-four hours.

I had missed my shift while in the hospital, and nobody knew where I was except that I was not at work. I must have gone back to sleep because two NCOs stood beside my bed when I awoke again and opened my eyes. Glenn from the day shift and Bill from the night shift were beside me. As I opened my eyes wider, looking at Bill, I could hear him ask the nurse on duty what had happened to me, and she said, '*Peanut butter.*' With disbelief on Bill's face, he repeated those words, '*Peanut butter?*' The nurse said, '*That's right, peanut butter.*' I told him, '*You know those cookies you all said were snickerdoodles? Well, they weren't. They were peanut butter!*' Neither of them had ever heard of anyone allergic to peanut butter until now. And this became a running joke at any party I attended after returning to D-M.

I was released several days later and authorized to return to duty. Some of the guys had already gone back to D-M. They had left before discovering what happened to me and my disappearance. One crew chief had decided to spread a rumor that I had left the base and shacked up with a girl. I believe that story may have made it to Pam.

I first worked with this man, who spread a lie about my disappearance shortly after arriving at D-M. He was my trainer. His job was to acquaint me with the DC operations and the differences between this aircraft and the HC and the C type 130s I have been on. Soon after being taught, I realized he knew less than I did about aircraft. He knew little about the C-130 aircraft, and I feared anything he touched and showed me.

He lacked knowledge of the functions of the DC-130, but the unit was short-handed in experienced crew chiefs. I was new to this aircraft and trusted him initially, thinking he knew what he was doing.

Landing gear struts on a C-130 aircraft are the components that provide support and cushioning during take-off, landing, and taxiing. These struts are part of the aircraft's landing gear system, responsible for absorbing the impact when the plane touches down and cushioning it from the landing force. They are designed to handle the immense weight of the aircraft.

The struts also consist of a hydraulic system and shock absorbers that compress and release as the aircraft lands, dissipating the kinetic energy generated during the landing process. Landing gear struts play a critical role in ensuring the safety and stability of the C-130 during its critical phase of flight, contributing significantly to the control of a safe landing.

To earn certification in the strut bleed process, the technician had to observe me conducting an actual strut service. He would first demonstrate the hydraulic right main strut bleeding procedure to me.

He requested wire cutters to remove the safety wire from the Shrader valve jam nut. He proceeded to use the crescent wrench to loosen the 'B' jam nut from the valve. I intervene, questioning his actions. He insisted that this method was standard for bleeding the main strut, contrary to my experience of never bleeding by removing the Shrader valve...

Realizing the potential issue, I stopped him before disassembling the Schrader valve assembly from the strut. I tried to take charge of the bleed. Despite my intervention, he persisted. I left the wheel well and promptly informed the flight line supervisor of the situation. The supervisor inspected the procedure and removed the trainer from the task. Subsequently, the supervisor approached me, inquiring about my knowledge of strut bleeding, and upon my affirmation, directed me to complete the job.

The technician, who had almost caused significant damage, was officially reprimanded and temporarily reassigned from the flightline for further training. He was relocated to a non-power age pool.

Because I had reported him to the line chief, he thought I had ruined his career. The sad part was he and his wife lived next door to us in the apartments. He often threatened me with revenge with *'Someday I'll get you back.'* But I just shrugged it off.

Then, the rumor he started after he left U-Tapao and I was in the hospital was that I had shacked up with someone downtown. I did not know the story during my TDY and only found out much later. Word had gotten off base. I never spoke of my peanut butter attack over there to Pam; maybe I should have.

This TDY at U-Tapao began okay. I receive mail regularly from Pam. But after a month and my hospital stay, her letters stopped coming. I could not write to her in the hospital because I had one I-V in each arm. When I was out of the hospital, I sent her a letter asking her to send money. I had just enough to use until she sent me a check.

I had not written to her and told her about the hospital stay as I did not want to worry her.

A week passed, and I did not receive any response from her. I wrote to her again and waited, but now I was out of cash and had no checks. When Billy learned I was not eating meals, he offered to cover my cost until I heard back from Pam. Billy was a good friend and supervisor during this TDY. He had loaned me the money to cover all my meal expenses for about two weeks until I was sent home on an emergency leave.

Someone unknown to me from the squadron requested that the Red Cross go to our apartment to see if Pam was okay. I understood that they sent out TSgt Henke, the squadron's primary contact for Pam. After work, he went to the apartment when he thought she would be home. When she did not answer the door, he left a note for her to call him when she returned. No call was received. The following day, the Red Cross was asked to go out and saw the note was removed. All I knew was that the Red Cross visited the apartment and thought I best come home. They reported their findings to the squadron and the commander. From there, TSgt Henke was asked by the commander to visit the home, and he did. When he got back, he reported his findings to the commander. Another memo from the 100th commander to the 99th commander in Thailand said there may be a problem at home and that I should be sent back as soon as possible.

Still in U-Tapao, and working on the flightline, Sergeant Hinkley came out and told me to get into the truck as I was to report to the commander's office. I was in the middle of a pre-flight before our shift change that morning. When I arrived at operations, I walked through the orderly room with many eyes on me. Strange, what is going on? When I finally made it to the commander's office I reported in, the commander said that the Red Cross requested that I be sent home immediately as there was a problem. Not informed of the problem or the situation, Master

Sergeant Hinkley picked me up from the operations building and drove me back to the hooch so that I could pack. He waited at the hooch as I packed. A C-5A was diverted to U-Tapao to take me to Clark Air Base in the Philippines. When it landed, Master Sergeant Hinkley whisked me out to the sitting behemoth. It had stopped at the end of the taxiway near the beach. They only shut down the two engines on the aircraft's port side (left), and I found out I was the pax that would be riding on it. Other than a loadmaster, I was the only person sitting in the back at the top of the cargo bay. Any seat was available to me for the next four hours to get me to Clark Air Base in the Philippines. Once at Clark, I was processed on a commercial airliner back to San Francisco and then to Tucson.

When I landed in Tucson, Pam met me at the civilian airport. I must have called Pam from San Francisco, but I cannot remember how she was contacted about my arrival. She was surprised to have heard that I had come back early.

The next day, I reported to the squadron and was given a week off to spend time with my family. Pam never asked why I had returned early. Nothing seemed wrong when I saw her at the airport, and she acted normal. Everything is fine; at least, I thought it was. So, we continued our everyday life as if nothing had happened. I said nothing about my hospital stay for the peanut butter cookie I didn't eat but tasted. I never knew about the rumor told to her by the former neighbor from our old neighborhood.

Buying our First Home

FROM THE BOB CROTHERS COLLECTION-House on Mormon Drive

In May, the former neighbor next to us at the new apartments moved into a recent home close to Pantano wash. I have heard that more of the guys from the unit were also buying homes there. I started thinking that Pam and I should buy a home. After all, this was a stable tour, with only TDYs.

Pam and I discussed the possibility of owning our own home. And we agreed that we should drive out there and look at it. It was a newly developed area, and the homes ranged from sixteen thousand to nineteen thousand dollars.

Pantano Wash was a dry riverbed most of the year, but in the spring, it is a raging river from the snow melting in the mountains nearby. There was not much in the area, just desert, but it was close to the base.

That side of town was not even built up with conveniences like gas stations, food stores, or transportation. We would have to drive several miles from the house to the nearest gas station.

One Sunday afternoon in early June, we drove to the area and looked at the development. I don't think we intended to buy that day; we just wanted to see what our friends were buying and what was offered.

All the homes were single-family homes. We sat in the car and discussed the area, as it was very remote. Then we talked about the style of the homes we saw from the car. We looked at each other and then decided to go in and walk through the models.

It was just another sweltering day in Tucson for the month of June. We got out of the car, approached the sales office, and went inside, where Pam and I were greeted by one of the salespeople. He told us about the company and then showed us all the renditions of the homes available for purchase. It looked like a beautiful place to live, and the area map showed plans of other developments around us, a new shopping mall and a new city park across from the development. Then he showed us the way to the model homes, where we could walk through all the models.

We toured each of the models. As we did, we talked about what we liked and didn't like about each one. A couple of them went through fast as they did not catch our eye. There were the pluses and minuses of each home we liked. When we stopped at the last one, we knew immediately that this was the home for us. We both liked what we saw in front of us. We went inside and walked around, and we wanted this home.

We returned to the sales office, met with our sales representative, and told him about the house we liked. He said they had planned to build that style on larger lots, and we had to find a lot we could build on. We found the last sizeable lots for our home. We chose a corner lot from where the city planned to build a new park. It was one of the largest lots in the development on Mormon Drive. Pam and I agreed this was what we wanted, and we could live in the area for the time we were stationed here.

The cost of this lot was a little more than the others because of its size. However, we did not want a standard-size lot as we thought they were small, and the corner lots were more prominent and had more backyard and side yards than the standard lots. Pam should have what she wanted as she sacrificed things to be with me and the Air Force. Since I would be on TDYs once or twice a year, Pam needed a home, a place that allowed her to be without noisy neighbors on the side of another wall.

The salesperson also told us some names of those from D-M who have purchased homes in the area. One of those owners we knew. And we wondered how they could purchase the home. We bought what we thought was one of the most desirable lots in the development. Next, we had to sit down and pick out the appliances we wanted in our new home.

Our home would have one full bath and a three-quarter bath in the master bedroom. It was funny that we would have our bath in the master bedroom. As kids growing up in our family homes, we had just one bathroom, and we learned how to share that one bathroom.

Now that we are buying our first home together, our master bedroom is more prominent than our apartment bathroom and childhood home. I could hardly wait to chase her around in our new home at night.

Next, we chose to have a laundry room instead of a workbench. So, we ordered it with a new washer and drier. No more driving to laundromats each week.

The kitchen counter colors were avocado green. All appliances were electric, and a built-in dishwasher was included. The kitchen had ample space for our new kitchen table and chairs. No dining room.

A large sliding glass door led out to the backyard from within the kitchen, with a window over the sink looking into the backyard. I told Pam I would build a fence around the yard to help keep others from entering the backyard. Also, that was where the trash pick-up was. We even had enough room for a swimming pool if we wanted.

The carpet went throughout the house. It was a 70's shag carpet, light in color, and I painted the walls to match before moving in.

We were just starting our life in 1973. We were excited about purchasing our first home at ages twenty-one and twenty-three. I never imagined that at our age, we would be homeowners. I'm sure we would not have been able to buy a home in our hometown in Massachusetts had we stayed there. I was happy to have been able to provide this for her.

We continued with the process of completing the purchase of our home. To purchase the house, we used the VA. This required no down payment. Once we completed all the paperwork, which took up most of our Sunday afternoon. When we finished and sealed our purchase with a handshake from the salesperson, we left and went to The Village Pizza Parlor for a celebration dinner. How ecstatic I thought we were. Pam said she was excited about this, and she was. But looming in her mind, other things were playing on her thoughts. I thought Pam was happy. Something was bothering her, and she kept it inside for several more months.

I was excited and could not wait to tell my parents the good news. However, I never did. Our home was purchased on June 21, 1973, and it would be ninety days before we would close on the property.

A week after all the paperwork was sent to the VA, we received written notice that they approved us for the home. Now, all we had to do was wait. During the next several months, while the house was being built, I would stop by after leaving the base to see how much work had been done each day.

I am unsure if Pam visited the site during the building stage. I would like to think she did and may have walked through it. But, if she didn't, it may have been because of the lingering decision she was about to make: will she stay with me or leave.

I watched the progression of our home being built almost every day. It also gave me a chance to have corrections made when I spotted the need. And I reported many things to the office that I thought were incorrect.

We received a notice in the mail telling us that the house would be ready for us to move into by the middle of September. I sensed something was wrong between us. She must have been struggling with her decision, or the other man she was seeing may have pressed her to remove herself from me. Though we continued to go out to the movies, visit Duane and Sally, and have several parties at our friends' homes on base, she was not the Pam I knew nor the Pam who came with me. I must be doing something wrong!

Our time together had been decreasing with each other. Pam was going out more, visiting our former neighbor from the first neighborhood we lived in by the university. Occasionally, when Pam was visiting our former neighbors, I would spend time helping Duane and Sally with their home projects.

Pam's Sudden Departure
An Emotional Roller Coaster Ride

Pam's personality really changed in the latter month of August. One night, returning from work to our apartment, she packed her clothes and was ready to leave me as I entered. Pam left one month before the house would be ready to move in. She was just leaving and had given me no reason as to why!

As she left the apartment, I stood in the doorway and watched her go, knowing that nothing good would come from this for me.

Pam would return to the apartment a couple of days later only to gather the items she had left behind that were hers. All the furniture stayed. She left her apartment key on what we referred to as the dining room table.

At first, I was very bitter toward her, more hateful. I learned where she went and drove over there often after my midnight shift. I would sit in the car and watch her apartment for hours to see if she would come out where I could approach her and talk to her.

I was not pleasant to her whenever I called her, but I mellowed out after a while, a long while. I would ask her if she could come over and talk when I saw her. She would not.

I called Pam's mother, or she called me, but during our conversation, I told her that Pam had left me. In another one of our talks, her mother expressed concern about Pam, suggesting something was wrong.

A week after Pam left, I got another call from her mother. I ended the conversation before we finished speaking. I had enough blame. What did I do to make her leave? She has a house being built. A home, not having to live in an apartment while we stay here. I never contacted her family for the remaining years in Tucson.

I believe her family found solace in her decision, akin to my choice, separating her from them. When asked about the situation, I found it difficult to navigate conversations without alluding to Pam's involvement. Whenever her name escaped my lips, tears welled up uncontrollably.

I lost my appetite for several weeks, and sleeping in the same bed we once shared was difficult. As I lay on our bed, my mind was continually active with thoughts of Pam. I even had to get rid of her pillow soon after she left. Some nights were so bad I ventured out to her new place, where she was now sleeping with someone else.

Pam had, I thought, hostility toward me. There was madness in her voice when I saw or spoke to her. I may have brought that on myself with some calls to her. One night, I received a call from Pam's new boyfriend, and he made several threats against me, though he never did carry out any of his threats.

Then, one night, around 8:00 p.m., while living in the apartment, the Tucson Police showed up at my door. They told me to stop bothering Pam and to move on with my life, as she wanted to be left alone. *'What was it I was doing?'* I asked. *'Harassment!'* I was told. The tall policeman at my door said a few more things, and I just looked at him and shook my head. He left with the final words, *'If you don't and I get a complaint, I'll have to arrest you the next time we come out.'*

I heard from the finance company that would be giving us the loan. They told me the closing date for the house. I contacted Pam, as she was still in the area, and told her **she had** to be there to close the house.

Entangled Hearts

The closing on the home took place on September 19, 1973; Pam, who had been absent for a month, arrived at the title company as she had promised to sign the papers for the house on that very day. Her appearance was my final hope that she would return.

When Pam graced the office that day, it was as if time had stood still since our high school days working at D'Amato's. Her arrival was nothing short of enchanting. As she stepped out of the car, surrounded by an air of elegance and accompanied by her entourage, it was evident she had adorned herself in a new attire for the occasion. Seeing her in those hot pants was breathtaking; her beauty was always spellbinding. It didn't matter what she wore or how simple her outfit was; she radiated grace and allure. Her new partner was fortunate to be with her. My eyes were on Pam; she embodied sheer, mesmerizing beauty.

She was cordial towards me that day. We walked into the office and went into the room together to sign the papers on the home, leaving her protectors outside. How did you learn to hate me so suddenly? One day, I thought our togetherness was sound and happy; next, you're gone. During the closing, she signed the documents without saying anything to me. She asked if we were done and was told yes.

Then stood up and left. I suppose everyone in the room thought it odd she was going with someone else. I stood there, watched her walk out, and my eyes followed her to the car. As I watched her drive away, I thought, *'She just gave up all of this, and for what?'* What happened to us? I just lost the one person I loved since high school. Now I had this new house; she had a new boyfriend. I would move into the house, but it would never have become a home without her.

I pulled up to the house, its familiar silhouette against the sky, a silent witness to the turbulence within me. I lingered in front, imagining Pam's arrival, hoping for a glimpse of regret in her eyes. But the street remained empty, devoid of any sign of her.

Memories flooded my mind, swirling like an incessant storm. I couldn't shake the haunting recollection of our departure from Massachusetts. Questions plagued me, each one a sharp thorn of doubt: What had triggered her departure? How long had this unraveling been underway? The weight of my own perceived failures pressed upon me. I struggled to understand where I'd faltered. With a heavy heart, I stepped out of the car, the click of the door echoing in silence. The familiar creak of the front door seemed to mock my shattered hopes as I stood on the threshold, tears blurring my vision.

At that moment, I longed to recreate the dream we once shared. Or were they just my thoughts and dreams? Imagining Pam in my arms, I yearned to carry her across the threshold, symbolizing our union. But all I could do was stretch out my arms to a space, echoing what was lost. With a heart heavy with grief, I crossed into what was to be our sanctuary, now a hollow empty shell without Pam by my side.

I found the house to be very lonely and cold. It echoed the loneliness I was feeling. But in another way, I was excited to be moving in. It would be a fresh start for me. It was a lonely beginning for me, but a fresh start! I would live in this house without her.

Living life without You

In the wake of Pam's abrupt departure, I found myself grappling with a turbulent storm of emotions. My initial instinct was to point fingers at the military, to hold it responsible for the void that had taken hold of my life. It was easy to cast blame on an external force, to believe that it had torn us apart. But deep down, I knew that this was merely a scapegoat, a convenient distraction from the real enigma that haunted me.

Pam had walked out on me, leaving behind a trail of unanswered questions that gnawed at my soul. Her departure had become a catalyst, transforming me into someone I no longer recognized. The once jovial and approachable crew chief had morphed into a brooding figure shrouded in bitterness. It wasn't long before my fellow crew chiefs, sensing the darkness that had consumed me, began to steer clear. My name became synonymous with hostility, and some refused to collaborate with me, fearing the unpredictable outbursts that led me to abandon my duties and storm off the flightline.

As time passed, the divide between my comrades grew wider. The camaraderie we had once shared, the squadron functions and lunches we had partaken in together, were now distant memories, fading like the vapor trails of a passing aircraft.

I searched desperately for someone or something to hold accountable for Pam's departure, for the inexplicable wedge that had been driven between us. Was it me, with my own flaws and shortcomings? Or had she found solace in the arms of a new love, someone who had stolen her away from me? The answers remained elusive, concealed behind the door she had walked through, leaving me in a state of perpetual uncertainty.

Struggles with Pam's Departure

The absence of Pam weighed on me like a leaden anchor, casting a shadow of despair over every aspect of my life. For the first time, the Air Force, which had always held a place of paramount importance, began to pale in comparison to the significance of Pam's presence. It gnawed at my soul, raising questions that clawed at the edges of my consciousness.

Was she walking away from us because of my chosen career path? Had I made the colossal mistake of not taking her back home when she asked me to? Would we still be standing strong together today had I brought her back to her home? Perhaps, in hindsight, I should have made the transition to the Air Force Reserves.

I used to believe that Pam couldn't bear the separation during my temporary duty assignments (TDYs). The truth was, I struggled with our partings. TDYs were an inherent part of my career, something I not only had to do but also something I found fulfillment in.

Could it have been the way we left Massachusetts to embark on this journey? I searched for any plausible justification, any explanation that would rationalize her departure from my life.

Day by day, I unwittingly sabotaged my own career, chipping away at my inner fortitude and eroding my self-worth with each passing moment. That day in August 1973, when she left me, marked the beginning of an endless evening of despair that haunted me relentlessly.

Sergeant Williams Heartfelt Talk

Pam's departure was a seismic shift in my life that tore at the seams of my being. My squadron, inexplicably patient, endured my deteriorating demeanor, a stark contrast to the dedicated NCO I once prided myself on being. I allowed neglect to seep into my routine-skipping formations, flouting uniform regulations, and carelessly disregarding responsibilities. Lunch breaks stretched into indulgent hours, often laced with alcohol, and I abandoned critical unit meetings, eroding the very core of my duties.

The breaking point arrived when I callously skipped a medical appointment, triggering a formal reprimand. My friend Billy had warned me countless times, but I stubbornly ignored his counsel. The dedication I once held dear was unraveling, slipping through my fingers like grains of sand.

It took Senior Master Sergeant William's intervention to jolt me from my downward spiral. He confronted me in the parking lot with disappointment and concern. He recounted my past valor and willingness to sacrifice for others. His words struck deep, stirring memories of a selfless past overshadowed by recent recklessness.

'Crothers,' he begins, 'you've strayed from the path expected of an NCO. Yet. Your history speaks of someone who went above and beyond for their comrades. Billy fought for your career, sacrificing his own to save yours.'

His words resonated, awakening a resolve buried beneath layers of self-destructive behavior. I realized I had to change or face the demise of a once-promising career.

The weight of Pam's absence lingered, but I knew sacrificing my career wasn't worth the sorrow. Williams made it clear that my squadron appreciated Pam, but my current trajectory would destroy everything I held dear.

Leaving the parking lot, I returned to my duties, seeking solace in the familiarity of the aircraft flight deck and the flight engineer's seat. Tears traced silent paths down my cheeks as I grappled with my shortcomings.

As our shift ended, Duane's concern broke through the solitude. His dinner offer echoed in the air, but my resolve held firm. I had promised to fulfill a promise to Pam, even in her absence.

Yet, as I stood in the parking lot, watching Duane drive off, a familiar pull tempted me toward the NCO club. I resisted, uttering, 'It's time to change.'

With a newfound determination, I turned away from the club only to return, redirecting my steps towards the club. Though it was time to honor my commitment to myself and the career I cherished, I had thought tomorrow I would start.

Resisting Change:
The Temptation at Twilight

I arrived at the club where I had few friends left. One of them asked me to come in and join them. It was another night of drinking for me. It was happy hour, and beer was twenty-five cents. Sitting at the club with the guys relieved me of those thoughts of Pam for those mere minutes. By 8:00 p.m., some guys started calling home to have their wives come to the club and pick them up. Several of them offered to drive me back to my house, but they lived in the opposite direction, so I refused.

Soon, everyone had left. I was the only one at the table, alone and drunk. I finished my final beer and stood up from the table as straight as possible. A *whew* with a wipe across my brow came from my mouth. I now had to focus on a path through the club toward the front door. Still, and most importantly, not to stagger as I walked from my table to the front door. The last thing I needed tonight was for the club manager to call the security police (SPs) to escort me to the base station. If they did, they would have contacted my commander. He would have notified the first sergeant and called my section chief, who had just talked with me earlier today. I would have had a fast trip to that Article 15 and my walking papers handed to me.

Sunset Sorrow and Memories

    I reluctantly pushed the glass doors open, venturing out into the scorching, oppressive air. The sun hung low in the sky, casting a fiery glow over the western mountains, a sight that would have once been perfect for Pam and me. Memories of our countless evenings together, watching these sunsets, flooded my mind, each one now a painful reminder of what I had lost.

I couldn't help but compare the breathtaking beauty of the sunset to Pam's radiant presence. The tears welled up, hot and relentless, coursing down my cheeks as I stood there, battling with the haunting memories of our time together. Deep down, I knew I had drowned my sorrows in one too many drinks.

Leaving the club, I trudged toward my car across the sweltering parking lot. I yanked the door open, and a wave of searing heat hit me like an inferno. I sank into the driver's seat, my skin burning against the plastic covers I had purchased to shield the fabric from my own misery. Long pants may have saved me from sticking to them, but they couldn't shield me from the agony within.

With a heavy heart, I started the engine and cranked the air conditioner to its maximum setting. I needed the cold air to numb the searing pain that consumed me. As swiftly as I had entered the car, I bolted back out, desperate for the frigid embrace of the air conditioning, a futile attempt to cool the burning torment of my soul.

I drove home on all the backroads, using Golf Link, to avoid the local police when I left.

Entangled Hearts

I skirted along the backside of the aircraft boneyard until I reached Pantano Wash road and managed to get home using that route. The drive seemed longer than usual but was not; there was a low chance of encountering the Tucson Police on this route. My whole drive home was all thoughts of Pam. As I listened to the radio, my feelings for her intensified. I started to feel anger toward her, and every sad country song that played made it worse.

I knew where she had moved to, and it would have been easy for me to drive there. Still, I was only one beer away from being placed in the city jail now that I was off base if caught, and my Air Force career would be over before my attitude could change. Add a drunk-driving charge to my counseling today, and the mess I would have had; I would have never seen the light of day for a while. Something Pam needed from me.

A Fresh Start Begins

Pam was gone, but not out of my memory. The memory of her smile, her laughter, and the way she used to curl up on the couch with a book in her hand and her legs tucked beneath her would linger for a lifetime. Pam and I had just finished closing on the house, a quaint little place with dreams of it being big. A home to raise our children someday and a home to live in while stationed in Tucson until we move back to Massachusetts. After I drove out and walked around it, admiring its potential, I headed back to the almost empty apartment.

The apartment had been our home for several months, where we'd shared countless joyful and challenging moments. But now, it was merely a temporary waypoint in my journey forward. In about two weeks, I would move out of the apartment and into the home Pam and I had dreamed of together. It was a bittersweet transition, filled with the echoes of her absence.

During these several weeks leading up to the move, I found solace in the house. I would drive over every day after work, eager to transform it into a place that felt truly ours, even if she wasn't there to share it with me. I painted the walls with warm, inviting colors, envisioning the life we'd planned together within these very walls. I installed a charming mailbox at the front to welcome us to a future of happiness and fulfillment. I did my best to make something out of the dirt they called a yard, planting flowers and nurturing the soil in the hopes that it would someday bloom into a beautiful garden.

As the moving day drew nearer, I rented a U-Haul truck, and my best friend Duane came over with his wife Sally to help me. Sally, always the organized one, efficiently packed all the dishes and glassware carefully, ensuring they arrived at the new house unscathed. Duane and I tackled the heavy lifting, loading the furniture into the truck with both the excitement of a fresh start and the weight of the past on our shoulders.

The last weekend of September was a blur of boxes, laughter, and a few tears. But as the sun set on the old apartment for the final time, I couldn't help but feel a sense of optimism. The house was waiting for me, full of promises and untold adventures. It was a place where I could rebuild my life, even if it meant doing so without Pam.

In the first week of living in the house, I threw myself into the task of making it our home. I painted room after room, each stroke of the brush carrying a piece of my hope and love. I hung curtains, with Sally's help, making the space feel cozy and warm. And I built an entire entertainment wall, envisioning the countless movie nights and cozy evenings ahead.

The house came with a washer and dryer, small luxuries that I had grown to appreciate. The first week I lived there, they were put to beneficial use, a reminder of life's simple pleasures, even in the face of loss.

Pam may have been gone, but her spirit lived on in every corner of the house. It was a place where memories would be made, dreams would take shape, and life would go on. And so, I settled into my new home; I knew that this fresh start was not just about moving forward; it was about honoring the love and dreams we had shared and finding my path in a world that had changed forever.

Departure and Depression

October arrived, and with it came the haunting specter of Pam's absence. Our communications had dwindled to nothing, and I had even lost sight of her whereabouts. I ceased my fruitless vigil near her residence, resigning myself to a life without her. Each night, I returned to the house we once were to share, only to find it devoid of Pam's presence, an echoing void that mirrored the emptiness in my heart.

Days were manageable, filled with the company of supportive friends who did their best to keep me occupied after work. They engaged me in activities and conversations, but as the sun dipped below the horizon, profound loneliness descended upon me. The nights were especially lonely, as were weekends when Pam's absence was most pronounced, and were a crucible of despair.

I tried to convince myself that I was holding up and coping with her departure, but deep down, I was drowning in a sea of melancholy. It felt like life itself had lost its luster without Pam by my side. The weight of depression pressed upon me, and I wondered if I could ever muster the strength to move forward.

My weekends were consumed by a relentless list of household tasks that cried out for attention. Improvements took up my time, but they couldn't fill the void left by Pam's absence. Even with the unwavering support of my friends, the pain and memories of Pam remained insurmountable during those lonely evenings.

As I navigated the tumultuous sea of emotions, I longed for a day when the echoes of Pam would fade into distant memory and I could truly begin to heal.

Suicide attempt

After I settled into the house, it lost its essence; it became an empty shell. Thoughts of Pam consumed me relentlessly. Despite my attempts, tracing her steps led to the stark realization that she had departed Tucson with her new partner.

Life took a relentless downturn after her departure. Now echoed with memories of our togetherness of finding and purchasing this home, haunting reminders of our shared moments. Pam is now an omnipresent fixture in my mind, her absence a constant ache that I couldn't shake.

One night epitomized the agony I had grappled with since her exit, and visiting the NCO Club highlighted the thoughts of self-harm. The battle against suicidal impulses became a nightly struggle within the confines of that desolated house. The darkness seemed to amplify the weight of her absence. What purpose did my existence hold without her? If she found it so easy to leave, what was the point in clinging to a life she seemed indifferent to?

Days blended into a blur of despair. Night after night, engulfed by solitude, my mind became a battleground for thoughts of ending it all. The relentless question persisted: what life did she now lead, and what scraps of existence remained for me without her? The conviction that living life without her was unbearable echoed ceaselessly, drowning out any glimmer of hope.

The night pressed on, a suffocating weight on my shoulders. Thoughts of Pam twisted and turned in my mind, an unending reel of memories and what-ifs. The kitchen table became a canvas for my pain, scattered with letters penned in desperation, the inked echoes of love slipping away.

In the dim light, I wrestled with the choice that seemed to loom more prominent with each passing moment. Anguish had a relentless grip on me, an ache so profound it blurred the line between love and resentment. I wanted her to feel the weight of her absence, to understand the abyss she left in her wake. The notes, my final testament to a love unreturned, lay strewn before me, each word a last testament to a hollow space she once filled.

My mind, a tempest of emotions, swung between sorrow and a simmering rage. The desire to comfort her burned within a violated mix of longing and fury. But she had already moved on, the distance between us more than just miles.

The clock's hands inched forward, marking time I wished would halt. It was now 11:30 p.m., a ticking reminder of life stalled, of an unbearable existence without her. My grip on the pen tightened as I finished the last words; a culmination of my heart poured onto paper.

I returned to the bedroom, a ghostly echo of what once held our dreams, and gathered those letters' my futile attempts at rekindling a flame that had been extinguished. Those papers felt heavier than ever, each sheet another testament to a love lost and a future shattered.

Living seemed an impossible feat. Yet, amidst the deafening silence of the night, a flicker of hope struggled to survive within me, a whisper that maybe, just maybe, there could be a dawn beyond this endless night.

I made my way back to the bedroom, the telephone rang, piercing through my despair. It was late, and I had never received calls this late in the evening. I was hoping it might be Pam calling and wanting me to come and bring her back home. When I answered the phone, the voice on the other end said, this is a recall, and I was to return to base immediately with enough clothes for thirty days TDY. Duty called and my responsibilities in Strategic Air Command (SAC) were suddenly paramount, despite the chaos within me.

Entangled Hearts

I packed my belongings hurriedly, but as I sat on the edge of the bed, I noticed the sleeping medication in my opened nightstand drawer. It was as if they beckoned me to take them. I swallowed the entire bottle, laid back on the bed, and welcomed the oblivion.

But my failed attempt at suicide was thwarted by an unexpected squadron recall. When I failed to respond, a concerned friend, Duane, reached out to his wife, Sally, who held a key to my house. Still living nearby, Sally drove to the house to see why I didn't respond.

When she arrived and saw the lights on, she came in using her key. She found me on the bed unconscious and my bags half-packed on the edge of the bed. She also found the bottle of sleeping aids and placed the empty bottle in her pocket. Now unable to awaken, she got concerned, dragged me out into her car, and took me to the Tucson Medical Center instead of the base hospital, where I spent the night. Sally remained with me at the medical center.

The next day, I was released. Sally drove me home without a word said, but an unspoken understanding developed between us. She called the squadron for me and told them I was sick, while they mistakenly believed it was Pam.

In the aftermath of that night, Sally became my close confidant, a steadfast friend who provided the support I so desperately needed. If Sally and Duane remained at Davis-Monthan Air Force Base, I knew that I had a lifeline, a connection to help me weather the storm of my emotions.

Struggles without her

After the darkest moment of my life, the suicide attempt, a haunting realization dawned upon me: Pam was gone for good. No matter how fervently I wished for her return, she had departed, vanishing into the depths of October, likely due to her grandmother's passing. Her departure was abrupt, devoid of any farewell to me. The naïve hope I clung to seemed foolish. For Pam had become an elusive specter. An unrelenting ache was now inside of me.

Despite the camaraderie of my friend, Billy, Pam's absence cast a shadow. I battled the relentless depression that clung to me, a ghostly reminder of her. I know I had to break from the shackles of my own misery, but my thoughts remained trapped in the melancholic refrain of *'Poor me!'*

FROM THE BOB CROTHERS COLLECTION

I thought I was on the mend. I decided that I wanted to host the 1973–74 New Year's party at my house. I wrote home to my mother for her recipe for blueberry bars. I remember when my mother made these blueberry bars and how much I loved them. Still, since Pam left, my parents did not know about her being gone or the house we purchased. I saw no need to tell them.

I had invited the entire squadron of crew chiefs to the party. I was told it turned out to be a great party! There may have been thirty to forty people at the house. The blueberry bars, one of my favorites from back east, were a hit. The women did not know any man could bake. I live by myself, and I had to learn.

I only made enough of the blueberry squares to last a brief time. Many of the guys' wives brought their party favorites, as well. Of course, I never knew how many liked peanut butter treats until that night, as many were on the table. Only those with me during that TDY knew of my peanut allergy episode. Bill and Anita ensured I avoided those with peanuts or peanut butter. I made sure that I did not kiss anyone who had eaten peanut butter at midnight.

As with most of our parties, the more we drank, the more the party drifted too outrageously. We played a few party games earlier that evening. One of them we played must have involved eggs. By the time midnight arrived, the eggs had covered the wall in the kitchen. Bill and Anita made sure things did not get too out of hand.

As midnight drew closer, you could hear gunfire and fireworks going off. I stepped out of the house to walk down to the corner. At first, I stood there looking up at the stars, wondering where Pam was. That's when my eyes swelled with tears. I yelled into the night, *'This house was for us both.'* Then I quietly said, *'To have other children while in Arizona. You took all that away from me! You took away my life,'* and then I shouted out nice and loud, *'Pam'* as if she would hear me and felt sorry for me. There would have to be a clean start to my life sometime in 1974, and I would learn to go with it alone.

After the party, I had one overnight guest, Jimmy, my good friend from Boston. He spent the night in the spare bedroom. Bill was going to drive him home, but I said Jim could spend the night in the extra room, and I would take him home the following morning.

The following day, when we awoke, Jim and I noticed the kitchen walls had egg yolk stains. We just looked at each other and laughed at the results. Then we got into my car, and I drove him back to his place. It must have been a letdown for him to have ridden in my car, as he had that rich Corinthian leather in his Cordoba. After returning to the house, I found some yellow paint and painted the kitchen wall.

For me, a rotation to Osan, South Korea, was in the coming months. Duane left for Osan before Christmas, and I was slated to replace my good friend. This will be my first long TDY since Pam left, and I moved into the house. Sally would look in on the house for me while I was away.

Midnight Shift Training Request

I felt a sense of weariness as we landed, and I stepped off the plane and back onto American soil after my TDY in Osan, Korea. The journey had been long, the time zones unforgiving, and the anticipation of returning home was weighted down by the knowledge of what awaited me. It wasn't the thought of reuniting with my family or catching up with friends that had me on edge, but rather the request that had been made waiting for me upon my arrival.

Billy Frederick, my colleague and a man I owed more than a few favors, had summoned me to a new challenge: the midnight shift. Dread coursed through me at the very mention of it. The midnight shift was the bane of my existence. The transition from day to night was always a grueling ordeal. Trying to stay awake during the midnight hours when the rest of the world was fast asleep was a task I despised. The day's scorching heat made it even more unbearable, and the absence of air conditioning in my house only added to my discomfort.

Yet, I couldn't say no to Billy. Not, after all, he's done for me during those turbulent times when Pam first left and my career hung in the balance. He had been my protector, my advocate, and now he was calling in a favor.

The reason for this unenviable shift became clear when Billy explained. Tech Sergeant Henke, our no-nonsense superior, needed an engine-run qualified crew chief to run engines after maintenance and train aircraft maintenance to fresh-faced troops out of tech school. It was a daunting task but one that held a certain appeal. The midnight crew had the early morning launches, the perfect opportunity to mold these newcomers into skilled crew chiefs.

With new troops on day shifts, the newbies were relegated to detail jobs, the less glamorous side of military life on the base. They mowed lawns and assisted in tasks unrelated to their AFSC (Air Force Specialty Code). Training opportunities were few and far between. Billy knew my penchant for teaching and the joy I found in nurturing the next generation of aircraft maintenance specialists. So, here I was, reluctantly agreeing to step into the midnight shift, knowing that my days would blur into nights and back again, all in the name of shaping the future of our unit.

While working the midnight shift, I would bring as many of our new maintenance trainees to the flight deck as possible if I ran engines that evening. If not, I put them in both seats to train them using the ground radio and simulated an engine run. Showing them how to find commercial radio stations they found to be fun. Then, play them over the speakers in the cargo bay as they would go back there and lay on the troops' seats until it was time to ready the plane for the flight engineer. In the meantime, I would transcribe the aircraft forms for that day's mission.

I would also have them call the ground control at night to get used to speaking to those who monitor us on the flight line when we run engines. I would let the tower know we were training. For most of those new troops, it was their first exposure to learning to use the C-130 aircraft radios, calling the control tower, and monitoring for passing by aircraft. For our new airmen, aircraft radios were a scary training. The training aircraft at Sheppard that most of us trained on was an old A model; we would be lucky if anything worked except for the number 3 fuel shut-off valve.

Entangled Hearts

FROM THE COLLECTION OF BOB CROTHERS-CLASS PICTURE JANUARY 1969

I would also train them to tune in to the local radio stations for music and play it over the speakers in the aircraft. I felt it would give them a better sense of their job in the aircraft field. I wanted them to know that you don't always get crap jobs when you're fresh out of school; I certainly didn't. However, a wild goose chase was not out of the question for me to do to them, and I would. I sent them out for things like retrieving a yard of the flight line or getting the prop washed before you wash the aircraft—none of which they could do.

My favorite prank was to send the new trainee out to get the spring tension of the exceptional release before a flight. Pilots would play along with us on this prank. The prank was nothing more than having the pilot sign off the aircraft acceptance block on Form 781. Seeing the new trainee go around to ask the flight line expeditor where they could get the spring tension for the exceptional release was funny.

Giving these young men and women a chance to see what we experienced crew chiefs do and what they are going to do once they complete their training to a five-level crew chief, I would hope, would entice them to study hard and learn all they could for the time they are serving in the military. Having them sit in on an engine run would change a new airman's attitude and commitment to their new career field.

Dating Again: Henke's Help

As Pam's absence lingered in my life, Sergeant Henke extended a helping hand to guide me through the void she left behind. With a generous gesture, he introduced me to his sister-in-law, fresh from Columbus, Ohio, and entrusted me with the task of showing her around during her initial months in towne. Those first few weeks were filled with moments of laughter and camaraderie as his sister-in-law, and I explored the city together. However, beneath the surface, I couldn't help but grapple with the undeniable truth: she wasn't Pam, and my heart still yearned for her.

Amidst the new friendship, I found solace in the shared dry humor that Henke and I both appreciated. In the midst of our camaraderie, there was a day when Henke, with his characteristic wit, broached the topic of Pam's departure. It was a moment etched in my memory, one that unfolded as we all sat in the truck one day on the flightline.

When Henke first learned of Pam leaving me, he joked about why she had left. He asked me one day, while in the truck,

'Crothers, do you know why your wife left you?'

Not sure where he was going with this, I answered no.

'Your tongue was too short, boy.'

Still talking, he said,

'If your tongue were longer, maybe she wouldn't have left you.'

I could hear Billy in the front of the truck say to Henke, '*That was bad.*' This means you should not have said that. But still, we all got a good chuckle out of it, including me.

Over the next few months, I had the pleasure of dating Henke's sister-in-law, and together, we've enjoyed some memorable experiences, including attending an Eagles concert and an Elton John concert.

TV Show Filming Adventure

In the heart of downtown Tucson, not far from where the life of another time, excitement brewed as a new television show was geared to be filmed downtown. A promising adventure awaited me. One that I unexpectedly found myself a part of. Assigned to the midnight shift out on the base, an unconventional twist in my schedule offered a rare chance to witness the magic behind the scenes of television production.

The show at the centre of all this was 'Petrocelli,' a gripping legal drama chronicling a New York lawyer's quest for a fresh start by launching a law practice in Tucson. Like myself, its premise seemed to echo my own life; just like the show's protagonist, I had recently rooted to Tucson alongside my love, Pam. I yearned for a renewed beginning for us together.

One Sunday morning, as I sat outside on the patio, soaking in another one of Arizona's warm and beautiful early sunrises and reading and perusing the local newspaper pages, my eyes fell upon a tantalizing opportunity. There was an opening call for extras to join the 'Petrocelli' TV show, and it seemed like the perfect chance to infuse some excitement into my midnight routine. Without much hesitation, I decided to join the show immediately after my night shift, ready to leap into this new, unexpected career path.

Pam was always the adventurer in our relationship, envisioning possibilities where I may have seen limitations. Perhaps this time, we would have shared a mutual passion for pursuing roles as extras in the television realm of allure and unknowns.

With her departure, a void consumed me. She was the one who saw potential. Perhaps, if she had stayed, we would have embarked on this journey together. Yet, these remain mere dreams of what could have been... I'll forge ahead alone, carrying thoughts of our missed opportunities.

Becoming an extra meant no monetary compensation, just a chance to blend into the show's background. But the prospect of possibly securing a more significant role in the show tickled my imagination.

On the day of the filming, after I had finished my shift out on the base, I arrived at the location the paper had told of, and the bustling atmosphere was nothing short of mesmerizing. The day was beginning; the sun was coming up over the eastern mountains, casting a golden hue across the city's landscape, as it hinted another scorching day ahead. The air buzzed with activity, a blend of sounds of city life involving the set. Cameras are everywhere, capturing every moment of this day. Newspaper crews from the local Tucson TV stations were filming the area, and reporters were trying to get interviews of those in the show.

In both my military role and as an extra on the set, I found myself in positions where directives governed my actions: when to move, what task to execute, and where to position myself. The irony struck me; whether in uniform or on the set, I was accustomed to awaiting cues, be they a command in the military or directions for a scene. I stood to act upon instructions given to me.

As the production crews bustled about, arranging and rearranging equipment in the city hall courtyard, a flood of memories surged within me. This very place held a bittersweet significance where Pam and I once stood, navigating the bureaucratic maze to legally add her to my checking account. Once the backdrop for our hopeful beginnings, the courtyard echoed with the nostalgia of a time long gone.

I closed my eyes, and suddenly, the scene came alive again. The gentle breeze carrying the fragrance of blooming flowers, the jasmine in the air, the sunlight painting golden hues on the cobblestone path- every detail etched vividly in my mind. But it wasn't just the picturesque setting; it was the vibrant joy of Pam's eyes, the laughter that resonated through the air, painting a portrait of our shared happiness in those early days.

Amidst the clamor of the crew's instructions and the hustle and bustle, I was lost in a world where Pam's infectious laughter drowned out the chaos. Each clatter of equipment being moved echoed the passing of time, a cruel reminder of the irreversible change. The ache in my chest grew as I longed for that bygone time, aching to reach out and grasp those fleeting moments once more. Yet, here I stood, surrounded by the ghostly remnants of memory, watching as the world moved on, heedless of the heartbreak swirling within.

Among the sea of people, I spotted trailers bustling with actors and crew preparing for the day's scenes. The scent of freshly brewed coffee wafted from a nearby craft services table, intermingling with the faint fragrance of sunscreen worn by those who had arrived early to beat the heat. Police personnel cordoned off the curious onlookers surrounding the makeshift courthouse set, their authoritative voices occasionally cutting through the din of excitement.

The familiar faces I hoped to find remained elusive despite scanning the crowd. Nevertheless, a surge of hope fueled my anticipation. I stood there eagerly awaiting my moment as an extra amidst this captivating spectacle.

I was fortunate enough to be chosen as a courthouse spectator, eagerly taking my place inside the courtroom. Unexpectedly, the director signaled for silence, and the scene commenced. However, it abruptly halted when the director called for a pause in filming. A person approached the director, who urgently requested someone switch off the air conditioner.

Puzzled as to why, those in the jury box were instructed not to wipe away any sweat while filming the scene, leaving us to wonder about the sudden request.

Sweating was strictly prohibited, with the air conditioning off and sitting under the hot studio lights. Do not wipe your brow! The only respite came when the director called out 'cut,' allowing us to wipe away the perspiration that had accumulated on our foreheads.

Despite the discomfort and unexpected challenges, the thrill of being part of this unique experience was immeasurable. It was a chance to step behind the scenes of a television show, a glimpse into the magic that brought the stories we all enjoyed on the screen to life. This one-time selection as an extra in 'Petrocelli' would forever be etched in my memory, an unforgettable chapter in my quest for a fresh start in Tucson.

Making changes in my life

Loneliness crept in like an unwelcome guest, lingering in the hollow spaces left behind when Pam and I drifted apart. The silence of an empty home grew too loud to ignore. During one of those solitary nights, the dull glow of the TV casting fleeting shadows, an unexpected beacon emerged from the screen advertisement for the 'Big Brothers' program seeking men willing to foster boys without fathers.

The idea tugged at something within me, a longing to fill the void and perhaps offer guidance to a young life in need. In a momentary impulse, I found myself at the threshold of applying to become a big brother. Surprisingly, the process moved swiftly, and I was accepted into the program within a fortnight.

Little did I realize the regulations awaiting me in this volunteer role. Rules governing everything from my personal life, including dating, to the commitment of time required. There were stipulations on how many hours I'd need to dedicate as big brother and the extent of involvement expected should the boy's mother seek my assistance, whether in education or behavior.

Once the Big Brothers organization completed its thorough vetting process, I was assigned a family yearning for a Big Brother figure. Initiating contact felt like stepping into uncharted territory; I had to reach out to the child's mother, gaining her approval before officially becoming her son's big brother.

My first little brother was from a Hispanic family. He was about twelve or thirteen and a rather bulky kid. But it did not matter; I was there because I wanted to be. We did the usual things as brothers, played ball, and had pizza after school twice a week. Occasionally, I would help with homework and other small items as needed. I was teaching the values and dealing with tough times. My little brother was the only boy in the house, with three sisters older than him. But as I thought more about this, I realized I was a big brother already, and what I was doing with the organization was not what I thought it would be. It was more of a strain on me to commit. Also, the kid was older than I wanted. But I continued to meet with him each week and some evenings.

Not long before, I got a call from the Big Brothers' office that the boy's mother did not think I was suitable for her son as I did not speak Spanish. The mom thought her son needed someone who was more Latino and someone who could speak Spanish. And she was right! I was not suitable for this young boy. I wanted a small boy I could help grow up and learn with him all the new adventures we could have together, like a father.

After a few weeks, another call came in asking me if I would like to try and see if this other family would be a fit. I declined and said that I was not right for the program.

A Desire for Children Denied

In the quiet recesses of my heart, Pam was an enduring presence, a cherished memory woven into my being from the days of our youth. Our love, vibrant and impassioned, lingered like an unspoken promise whispered by the winds of time. Fate, it seemed, had conspired to entwine our paths once more.

As we rekindled our connection, every shared smile, every familiar laugh, reignited the embers of a longing I had carried silently for years.

The desire for children with Pam wasn't a passing fancy or fleeting wish. It was an indelible yearning, an unwavering aspiration that whispered promises of a future together, brimming with laughter and maybe tiny footsteps echoing through the corridors of our purchased home. Imagining a family of our own, nurturing souls that bore pieces of our love, ignited an overwhelming sense of joy and anticipation within me.

With each passing day, my love for Pam would grow. So did the significance of this dream of mine of envisioning the love and support of our children. Flourishing under and with our guidance together as devoted parents. The thought of being a steadfast presence in their lives, shaping their futures with unwavering love and guidance, became an integral part of my life.

Our journey of growing together wasn't without its trials. Circumstances held us back from realizing this shared dream during the initial stages of our renewed bond. But despite the challenges, my desire remained resolute, a beacon of hope guiding me through the stormiest days.

The prospect of parenthood with Pam wasn't just a dream; it was a testament to my enduring love for her, transcending time and distance since our high school days. I longed for a future with her where we would nurture and watch our children flourish together. This future would intertwine our lives as profoundly and beautifully as possible.

Yet, fate, in its enigmatic course, chose a different path. Pam walked away, leaving behind the fragmented dream and the echo of a love that refused to fade within me. The love, the dreams, and the yearning for children persisted. Still, the possibility of sharing it with her dissolved, leaving behind a bittersweet ache of what could have been.

In the wake of her departure, the tender memories of our shared dreams turned bitter, etching a poignant ache in my heart for a love that would never fully bloom.

Chance Encounter Sparks Connection

Now working the day shift again, I ventured into a new chapter of my life without Pam, embracing a part-time evening gig as a security guard. In this nocturnal realm, I worked at Pinnacle Peaks, where we celebrated Pam's birthday dinner in November 1973.

As I frequented this convenience store near where I now live, I was captivated by a singular presence: a woman of remarkable allure who happened to be the cashier during the evening shift. Our initial exchange led to conversations, and I began unraveling her life's layers through those. Each night before my shift, I would find myself drawn to her register, our interactions becoming a highlight of my routine.

One particular evening, as the hours waned, we delved into discussions about our respective past, unveiling the reasons for our single status. I shared Pam's story while Susan confided in me about her ex-husband. During this heartfelt conversation, she revealed a part of her life that touched me deeply- her son, Charlie, who had been abandoned by her ex-husband. Susan's father, a loving but ailing presence, had stepped in to care for Charlie. However, her dad's health limitations meant he couldn't provide many of the things a five-year-old desires.

Having wanted children with Pam, I never had the opportunity to have them with her, for she had walked away shortly after we rekindled our love and put them into someone else's arms. Children meant a lot in my life. I had a soft spot in my heart to see no child grow up without a father.

After several visits to the store, I opened up to Susan about my attempt to be a big brother, a venture that didn't quite pan out. As I excused myself to use the restroom, two unfamiliar men wandered into the store, casually browsing the aisles. Upon my return, I immediately sensed something was off. A man stationed by the register and another lingering near the entrance, their behavior raising my guard. The recent string of convenience store and grocery store robberies echoed in my mind from my neighbor telling me that he was a victim of a robbery one recent evening. He was a night shift supervisor for the store he worked for.

I discreetly assessed the situation, drawing on past experiences, including my training in Vietnam. Clad in my security uniform, reminiscent of the Tucson Sheriff's attire, equipped with a 38 caliber revolver sidearm and loaded with 6 hollow points, I approached the front counter cautiously. Observing suspicious movements, I placed my hand on my weapon. Then, startling the intruders, I revealed my presence. A movement that sent them fleeing down the street.

Susan swiftly contacted the Tucson Police., Amidst the uncertainty, she implored me to stay until Law enforcement arrived. With my focus on ensuring her safety and assisting in any way I could, I remained by her side, ready to support her until the authorities took control of the situation.

When the Tucson Police arrived at the store, they took the information from her and me, and the officer stated that she was lucky I was with her. The officer told her they had been trying to catch these two guys and believed they were the two who had just robbed another store earlier that evening. I remained at the store until her father came at the end of her shift. I never made it to work that evening.

Several nights passed when she asked me if I would be interested in meeting her son. She told me that he wanted to meet the person who, as she said, "*Saved her mom.*" I told her, '*I would love to meet him.*' She asked if I could drive her home after work on Friday, and I said, '*Yes*'.

I arrived at the store Friday after her shift ended, and she was waiting for me outside the store. She got into the car and directed me to her parents' house. She got out of the vehicle no sooner than her son came barreling out and into her arms. I got out and stood there and smiled when I noticed her dad approached me and introduced himself. He began to thank me for saving his daughter's life and said that he and his wife were grateful I was there that evening for her. Her father and I walked over toward his daughter; she began to introduce me to Charlie. '*Hello, Charlie,*' I said, and he held his hand to shake mine. It took me by surprise, but I took his hand in mine and shook it. He asked if I were the one who saved his mom and said, '*I would not say I saved her, but I was there when she needed me.*' He thanked me and held onto his mother's waist. I was asked into the house and met Charlie's grandmother, who thanked me. I told her honestly that I did nothing; I just walked out of the restroom, that is all!

A few days later, she asked if I would like to be part of Charlie's life. I told her I had an upcoming deployment but would love to spend time with him until then.

Charlie and I spent as many hours together as we could before I left. We went to the airshow on base, and I put Charlie in the front seat of an F-4 fighter.

On another weekend, we went to Colossal Caves, which was fun. We discovered that these caves had been in some television shows and movies.

FROM THE BOB CROTHERS COLLECTION-Colossal Cave

Another time, Charlie and I went camping up to Mount Lemmon and camped at Rose Canyon Lake. Charlie and I tried our luck fishing. Able to bait the line for Charlie, I was never so glad not to have caught anything as I had no idea how to remove a fish from the line.

FROM THE BOB CROTHERS COLLECTION- Rose Canyon Lake

Church comes back into my Life.

Just before the next TDY, other changes came into my life. I started to attend church again. I found a similar church that was the denomination I grew up in and began attending Sunday church services.

I look forward to Sundays and church those next few months I had before I left on what would be my final TDY. Usually, after services, a few parishioners would get together and have coffee and donuts. I went to one of the service get-togethers and ran into one of our drone pilots. It surprised me that as small as our military unit was, I would run into another unit member or another member who was also of the same denomination as me.

I love attending this church as it looks like the one I grew up in back home. The inside organ pipes stood tall and majestic behind the pulpit. Large stained-glass windows adorn both sides of the church. Entry into the church, two massive doors hung and opened outward, allowing the parishioners easy access to the church and their pews.

As the year ended, members of the church choir group began to learn to play the bells for the Christmas service that they would have. I often stayed after the sermon and listened to the members play the bells.

Each member would be responsible for playing bells of different notes. Following the musical score in front of them, they would follow along and play their bells. I wished I had joined the church earlier as then maybe I too could have been a member of that group learning to play the bells.

Now that Pam has left me and the towne, I regret that we did not attend church together and wonder if that would have saved us from being apart. I just knew that her leaving me without reason still plagued me.

Final TDY

As 1974 grew closer to the end, I would be coming up with another TDY tour for 1975. I asked my section chief if I could pull it earlier so as not to be around for the holidays and spend it in the house alone. On his first enlistment, one of the married crew chiefs was scheduled to leave just before Christmas, and I was told to speak with him and see if he was willing to trade off rotations. I could not imagine a married man with children would not want to trade off TDY rotations during Christmas. And with that, I managed to trade rotations with him. I would take his cycle, and he would replace me 89 days later. The ghost of Christmas past would not be with me this year. I extended my TDY to complete two college classes I was taking.

During this time, TDY, I lost my house sitters, Duane and Sally. Duane had reenlisted and took an assignment to Germany for three years. My heart sank when he told me he and Sally would leave D-M for Germany. They were first going home for 30 days of leave before reporting to his new base in Germany. I could not be there to say goodbye to them as I counted on them for my support, but it was time for me to stop relying on them to listen to me whine over Pam a year and a half later. I was losing more than just one good friend; I was losing two; I would be missing two good friends.

Earlier this year, I tried to rent out two empty bedrooms, thinking that would be good to do while I went to Korea. Sally and Duane would still stop by occasionally to check on things. Sally would write to me and tell me how things were going at the house while I completed my TDY in Osan, Korea. When I returned in April, I went to the house and got there just as the sheriff drove up. A complaint of a loud party was called in.

I entered the house, followed by the sheriff. We sent every one of the college kids out and told them to get back to campus. I allowed the two students who lived there to remain the night.

The next day, I asked the renters to leave as they were no longer needed since they could obey the rules on the no-party request. I did not charge the two students rent living there; the deal was to take care of the house while I was gone.

In June, I went with one of our DC-130E aircraft to an air show, at March Air Force Base in Riverside, California, and spent the weekend there. I loved doing air shows as I got to show off my knowledge of the airplane and tell of its mission. And I love it when kids ask questions about how that airplane flies with the pylons under the wing while the drone is on the pylons or how you start those big engines. People love the cockpit of this aircraft, with all the switches, lights, and instrumentation, and its navigation station. Many questions were always asked when we allowed the people to see the plane. Sometimes, I would be asked to take a photo with them. Having the public on my airplane and answering their questions brought me joy.

Owning this house has not been a good thing for me. I should never have told Pam to come to the closing, and I should have walked away from the house. The house only brought thoughts of her the entire time she was not there. Christmas was coming, and I had no intention of spending it in that house without Pam. I decided she was not bringing me down this year.

I arrived in Thailand the day after Christmas. I missed Christmas this year as I left on the 24th and landed on the 26th of December.

After I had been at U-Tapao for a week, I noticed that the base education center had posted information on upcoming classes, so I went over and enrolled in two courses with the University of Maryland. I signed up for the FAA airframe license and my instrument pilot's exam. The courses were for six months, so I had to extend my tour to complete my classes.

Entangled Hearts

One day, while sitting on the aircraft ramp, reading my lesson for that night's class, I saw planes coming in. I had been on this aircraft all morning, and nothing had taken off. So, curiosity caught my attention. Two F5 planes came in simultaneously, and I put down the book I was reading to watch them land.

After they had landed, I looked to my right and saw not one, not two, but I could see several aircraft coming in as far as the eye out over the ocean at the end of the runway. What was going on? Surprisingly, I saw a C-119 land with all its cargo doors open. Now, I see not one pilot in the F5 cockpit but one pilot and three people. This went on for hours.

As I continued looking toward the ocean, I saw this ship coming over the horizon. As it drew closer, I could tell it was an aircraft carrier.

Because of its size, it was heading right up onto the beach. I am watching and seeing helicopters landing on the flight deck. Then, I saw several helicopters going over the side of the aircraft carrier. Later that day, I learned that the President of Vietnam had fled, and the new President had given up his country to the North Vietnamese. Vietnam has fallen. People were leaving South Vietnam, escaping from the NVA and Viet Cong to stay alive. Rumors had it that any South Vietnamese soldier caught by the NVA or Viet Cong would be executed on the spot for treason. Why wouldn't they take a chance to fly out of their former country into another country? And being free was a better option than death! It was the end of the undeclared Vietnam War on April 30, 1975.

In May, we were told about a merchant ship being seized just off the shore of Cambodia. We were unaware of what was about to happen on this base.

As I closed the aircraft I had been on, my flight chief pulled up and told us to get in the truck. We reported it to the fuel cell hangar. The word was that Marines would be coming in from Okinawa and using the fuel cell as a staging point. A staging point for what? We were not told the reason.

FROM THE BOB CROTHERS COLLECTION-May 1975

No planes could be in the fuel cell hangar, and any aircraft requiring fuel cell work was placed on hold or would take place out on the ramp. Since the base was on the ocean, the humidity was always 100 percent.

This would not be the first-time work that would occur on the ramp. We had portable air conditioners for this work.

Not long after the fuel cell hangar was set up, planes started arriving, and marines were getting off them and marching over to the fuel hangar. I began asking my flight chief about what was happening with the Marines' arrival. I told him my younger brother was in the Marines and out of Okinawa. He said that the Marines were coming in from Okinawa. Brian was in the 2/9 out of Okinawa, and when I heard that he was one of the units coming in, I would look for Brian in hopes of finding him.

Entangled Hearts

I stayed on the ramp that evening looking for him till 10:00 p.m. with no luck finding him. Somehow, I had not been in the right place at the right time to see him arrive. I went back to the hooch to get some sleep and would get up early the following day to search for him again. I will find him then.

At 5:00 a.m., I was up and walking from my hooch toward the hangar. I noticed helicopters lined up on the ramp as I approached the flight line. I walked a little faster to get to the hangar. As I neared the hangar, I saw formations of mariners marching out to those helicopters. I hurried to the ramp, went to the helicopters, and started my search for Brian. Stopping at each helicopter, I would call out my brother's last name in the hope of a response. Nothing! On several attempts calling out for Brian, an answer would come back, and I would be directed to another helicopter to look.

I finally reached the last copter on the ramp; a second lieutenant met me out on the ramp. I told him I was searching for my brother, and he called into the cargo bay of his helicopter for Brian. But again, no response. I stood there speaking with the lieutenant when he heard his radio crackle with the orders to mount up. The lieutenant responded to the call. He quickly turned and said he had to get going. I rendered a salute to him, wished him well, and said, be safe. He then hurried to the helicopter ramp and took his place onboard. I rushed to my plane as the helicopters were taxiing to the runway at the ocean end. They all flew from the end of the runway out over the ocean and towards Cambodia. I opened my aircraft crew entry door, walked to the ramp controls, lowered the ramp, and kept the cargo door down. I began my daily function checks of the aircraft systems. My aircraft had not flown for a few days, and we needed to run engines to circulate their oils. Not much activity has occurred since Vietnam fell on April 30th, 1975.

After finishing the aircraft inspection, I stood in front of my plane, turned toward the ocean end of the runway, and watched for the remaining few helicopters to take off. Dawn was just breaking over the water, and it was beginning to feel like it would be another warm day.

I then entered the airplane, walked to the back, and lowered the ramp, where I sat, thinking of my brother and the rest of those marines. In my head, I forgot all about Pam for the first time in a long time. It was not about her any longer but the safety of those Marines. And it was also about my brother, whom I worried about.

I said a silent prayer for Brian. I was torn that I had a brother in the service and was sent into harm's way. I swore this was my final enlistment when the time came to reenlist, as I could not have the two of us in another conflict.

The entire day, all my thoughts were on Brian. I knew he would be safe, as he was a marine, and his training was among the best.

During the rest of the morning, I waited in anticipation of the return of those helicopters. When they arrived, I ran down to them as each of them landed. I would watch every ambulatory Marine walking off the helicopter and every liter that was carried off to see if it was Brian.

When the last helicopter came back, and I had not found Brian on any of them, my flight chief pulled up to where I was standing, told me to get in the step van, and asked me if I had any luck finding my brother. I told him no. He told me to get some chow with him. We drove to my airplane, and I closed the ramp and crew door. I returned to the truck, and we went for morning breakfast at the NCO club, usually the best meal of the day.

Return to DM

My Final TDY ended in mid-June 1975, and I returned to D-M. The return flight was on a KC-135A aerial refueler out of Pease Air Force Base in New Hampshire. The crew taking it back was not from New Hampshire. The tanker crews would change out at each stop, and the new crew flew it to the next stop. All our flights were long and tedious, but not as long and boring as when I would ferry one of the DC-130s back to D-M. The difference, flying on a tanker back to D-M, was the number of stops made along the way. In the DC-130, you stopped on islands along the Pacific, allowing you to rest overnight on each Island. The tankers fly from Thailand to Guam to Hawaii and then to California, having fresh crews at each refueling stop. But with the DC-130, you had only one crew and would stay with the aircraft the entire trip to D-M.

Of course, it took many more flying hours to each stop of a DC-130 stop. Ask the crew chief if that bothered him or her, and they will say no! There was something about being a crew chief on a turboprop that you grew to love and sometimes hated. But one thing is sure: that aircraft would never let you down and get you home safely. And I was lucky to have had great crews that allowed me to fly this magnificent bird across the Pacific.

When our KC-135A reached March Air Force Base, we spent the night at a hotel downtown, as the on-base lodging was full. We would continue to DM the following day. The original Pease crew would pick up their airplane and ferry it back to their home station.

On this TDY, I had to leave my car outside our Flightline shack. It has been sitting there now for six months. For many of my earlier TDYs, Duane and Sally would take care of the car while I was away. If only

Pam had stayed, she could have been the one to pick me up on arrival. Yes, Pam still consumed most of my thoughts after two years.

When we landed at DM, we disembarked the aircraft, and my flight chief, Billy Frederick, was the first to greet me. Billy had returned from his TDY eighty-nine days earlier. Billy now standing at the foot of the air stairs, waiting for me like a rock star. I heard that familiar voice shout *Bobby C*, as I was known to him. Billy established my nickname as Bobby C while stationed in Bien Hoa Air Base, Vietnam. There were two of us with the same first name there. So, Billy decided to use Bobby C for me and Bobby P for the other. At DM, he once again ran into that problem with Bobby Gaskell. He quickly became Bobby G.

Bill welcomed me home, loaded my bags into the step van, and drove me back to our section, where my car was parked. He asked me if everything was good, and I told him I was okay. I said Bill, I made some novel changes in my life and accepted that Pam was and is now gone. Bill responded, ' *I'm glad to hear that, Bobby C, but sad that she is no longer with you!*' Then he asked if I would need any help at the house, and I said no, I would be fine. '*Duane left you a message in the crew lounge*,' he said, and I told him I would get it later as I just wanted to get home. So, he continued to drive me out to the parking lot.

I removed my bags from the truck and threw them into the car's front seat. Bill waited until I started my car. It has been idle for the last six months, and I wondered if the car would start up. It did!

It was now summer in Tucson, and summers in Tucson were blistering hot. It was common to see extreme temperatures inside cars, some reaching 140 degrees Fahrenheit. I would turn the car air conditioner on after I started the engine and then roll down the driver's window. I sat there for several minutes, and then thoughts of Pam returned as I recalled the first time I came back from my TDY; she was there to greet me. She was also there to tell me about the dent in the rear bumper. I never had it fixed; I wanted it there as it was part of Pam.

Entangled Hearts

FROM THE COLLECTION OF BOB CROTHERS-Pams' dent 1973

Staring out the car's window and imagining Pam here to pick me up, I got inside the vehicle once it cooled down and grabbed the steering wheel, hoping not to burn my hands. I put it into the drive and headed for the back gate and home.

I stopped the car and parked just before I reached the house. I sat there just staring at the home we purchased. In my mind, I was seeing Pam in the front yard. It's funny how heat plays with your mind.

I pulled up the driveway, and as I did, I noticed a large paper note taped to the front door. Had Duane or Sally placed that there? But then Bill said he left a message in the flight line crew room. That was odd, and I could not imagine why someone would leave a note on the door.

As I got out of the car, I could see my mailbox had mail spilling out of it. That, too, was odd as I had stopped the mail for the time I was going to be away. Later, I discovered the mail stopped the first 90 days and started up again while I was on my second eighty-nine days.

I grabbed the mail and walked up the driveway to the front door. On the door was a sheriff's notice. As I read the note, it stated that the house had been abandoned and was going into foreclosure.

I pulled off the notice and tape and opened the front door. Warm air rushed out, and with it, the smell of foul air. I threw my bags in the front room and opened all the windows. Then, I turned on the swamp box to circulate the air. The unit did not run; I thought nothing of it then. Then I walked into the kitchen. That is when I found out that my electricity was turned off. The stench was coming from the refrigerator. I opened the refrigerator door quickly, nearly passing out, and gagged at the smell from within it! It was worse than the smell from our honey bucket on the aircraft. I unplugged the refrigerator, pushed it right out the patio door into the backyard, and let it sit until I could find time to get rid of it.

After I had settled in and most of the smell was gone from the house, I read all the mail, which were all payment requests. I took my checkbook on this TDY, my gas and electric bill statements, and mortgage coupons. I knew I had to send payments during this TDY as I had no one to check on the house. Sally, who used to send my payments in from her home, was gone. Duane and Sally cleared the base three months ago. Sally had access to my credit union account (she was now acting as Pam) if she needed to pay for anything during my absence.

After spending the rest of my day reviewing all the mail, none from Pam, I organized myself to see what had happened since I was gone.

The water was still connected to the house, but the water heater was not working as it was electric, which had been turned off. Knowing that, I still decided to take a shower. The water was refreshing as the house was sweltering.

After I finished my shower, I decided to go out and get something to eat. I went to the Village Pizza for dinner. Now that I am back, those thoughts of Pam have come back. Here at the Village Pizza was the final place where we were happy as a couple when we celebrated the purchase of our home.

Returning to the house, I kept all the windows open and hoped for some sort of breeze to get some sleep. As I lay in bed, my thoughts of Pam returned, reminding me of my first night here without Pam. I lay awake thinking of her and bashing her for leaving then. As did that night, I tried to commit suicide so that I would never think of her again.

The next day, I got up early, sorted through all the mail from the credit union, and then drove there. I had money in the account, lots of money in there. There was a problem. I had to find out why I had money in that account and what had happened. I spoke with the bank manager and told him the situation. He took all the information and the check numbers and said it would be a couple of days before they knew anything. In the meantime, I contacted the mortgage company to see how to stop the foreclosure. I was on the phone for two hours, telling my story and giving them the check numbers I sent to pay the mortgage. It did not do me any good as they had to physically look everything up, which would take a couple of weeks. In the meantime, the process of foreclosure continued.

The house was hot, and the electric meter was removed. I could not live in this house with this heat. I contacted my friend Billy and told him what had happened. He would do what he and Anita could to help me through. I had a week off before I had to go back to work. The house is now in foreclosure. I await the bank's advice about my plea to save it.

Not one payment I sent from Thailand made it to the bank where they were sent. I went to the electric company and paid the bill, and they sent someone out, installed the meter, and restored my power.

Entering the home to be for Pam and me, my mind was ablaze with every evil thought I could have of her. This would not have happened had she been with me. I could do nothing now except wait until I heard back from the mortgage company.

I drove to the NCO club on base, where I could get a beer and have lunch. When I arrived at the club, I had settled down and was not mad now at Pam. I decided to skip the beer and have lunch with iced tea. The air conditioning in the club made it comfortable enough to relax, watch TV, and nap before I had to return to the house.

Once back at the house, I cleaned the refrigerator to remove the smell and moved it back into the kitchen.

Now that the swamp box was working, this helped freshen the home and cool it down a little. The swamp box was the poor owners' air conditioning.

After I finished the refrigerator, I called the loan company on the furniture, as they claimed no payments were made. I spoke to the loan officer, and while listening to him, I thought, *'What am I doing? Why do I want to keep this furniture?'* The loan officer gave me several options to get caught up on past payments. One was to surrender the furniture. I told the loan officer I sent payments, and the credit union was getting copies of the cashed checks. Still, they wanted the money by next week. So, I decided that they could have the furniture and surrendered it!

I received a call from the credit union. They informed me that they found no canceled checks. *'But where did my checks disappear, too?'* I asked. Then they told me my checking account had no withdrawals except the NCO club in Thailand, on cash drawn out for my personnel expenses. How can they get those checks, but no one got any of the checks mailed from the base over there?

I called the mortgage company again and pleaded with them to see if they could stop the foreclosure. They told me it was too late, and that I should have contacted them earlier. Had I known while overseas, I could have reached base legal for help. I went to the base legal aid and told them of my problem. Again, another lecture, as there was nothing anyone could do. I should have had another backup plan, legal said. Someone here could have sent payments for you, they said. I told them *I did until Sally and Duane were sent to Germany while I was gone.* No matter how often I told them of my loss, they were only sorry, and I should have a better backup plan before the next TDY.

The only friend left was Bill, but he was raising a family, and he had his struggles with his two older teenage daughters.

Later in the week, the finance company came for the furniture. The store manager arrived and backed up to the patio doors for the furniture. He informed me that he was sorry they had to remove all the furniture in the house. The manager, a former service member, understood my situation and had seen it before when he was in the military. As he said, it is nothing unusual to see. He also told me he made sure I would not have a balance to owe. And with that, I helped remove the furniture from the house. As we removed the furniture, it was like saying goodbye to Pam. I hope it will help me say goodbye to Pam forever now.

In the house, empty of all the furniture Pam and I purchased, only a few items remained with me. Now six years old, a TV, a few sheets, blankets, a radio, pots, pans, China, and silverware. I spent the rest of that week sleeping on the bedroom floor with the sheets I had.

I was almost homeless. I needed to find a new place to live. I found an apartment close to the base and moved into a studio apartment. The studio came furnished, which was a significant help; the last thing I needed was to buy furniture. I lived in this apartment until October 1976.

Moving from the 100th to the 355th

I worked long and hard to prove that I put Pam in my rearview mirror while still with the 100th OMS and to prove that the past was in the rear. Pam was never the problem of my self-destruction. It was me! Still, the commander was not convinced that Pam was no longer a liability to me, as I was not worthy of receiving my next promotion, and he turned it down. So, in December 1975, I requested to be transferred to the 355th, along with the DC-130A models.

I was well-trained in both the DC-130E and the DC-130A. And took on the responsibilities awarded to most E-6 and above. My EPRs (enlisted performance reviews) were exceptional. My Flight Chief wrote, '*Sgt Crothers was frequently observed with his performances as a DC-130E crew chief, and I am impressed with his enthusiasm, technical competence, and ingenuity in accomplishing complex tasks assigned to him.*' He even added that I was an asset to the organization. I trained as many of the new crew chiefs as I could.

When I requested to be sent to the 355th, MSgt Frederick was reluctant to let me go. But I insisted I wanted to be sent to TAC and the DC-130As.

I wrote my request letter to my Supervisor, Senior Master Sargeant Williams; it read;

'*I am writing to formally request my transfer to the 355th, specifically to work with the DC-130A models, and to share my eagerness to contribute to their success in this new mission. I noticed that you have been mainly sending inexperienced crew chiefs who either never worked on the A models or have limited time on them. This is unfair to the new unit; thus, my request.*

In addition to my request for tenure at the 100th OMS, I dedicated myself wholeheartedly to the mission. In return, it had cost me the loss of someone I was very much in love with. I have demonstrated adaptability and commitment to this unit despite facing challenges upon my return from Thailand in June 1975. I was steadfast in my efforts to overcome obstacles in the past and contribute positively to the unit.

My flexibility was evident when I transitioned to the 3rd shift and later resumed my responsibilities during the evening shift, where I mentored and trained numerous new tech school graduates.

Reflecting on my journey, I've come to understand and take responsibility for any personal obstacles that might have affected my professional trajectory. While my association with Pam might have raised concerns, I have actively worked to ensure that it did not impede my commitment to the mission or my dedication to growth and improvement.

I believe my tenure at the 100th OMS has equipped me with invaluable skills, knowledge, and experience that will undoubtedly contribute to the success of the 355th. I am eager to leverage these skills and my unwavering commitment to excel in a new environment and further contribute to the squadron's objectives.

I am enthusiastic about the prospect of joining the 355th. I am confident this transfer will provide personal and professional growth opportunities.

I am requesting an immediate transfer to the 355th to prove that I am dedicated to my profession and deserve the promotion I was denied.

Sincerely,

Sgt Robert A. Crothers USAF'

I arrived at my new duty station in January of 1976 and asked to be placed on the second shift. A tech sergeant who had just returned to the Air Force after having been a civilian for several years had just arrived in the unit.

I wanted the second shift as that was the maintenance shift for the aircraft. And I figured this new Tech Sargeant could use my knowledge of the DC-130s. Most of his crew chiefs were those I had just trained on the DC-130E aircraft. I was the most experienced crew chief to help him get acquainted with this aircraft.

The planes flew most of their training missions during the morning and afternoon. Within a week of working the second shift, I obtained my engine run certification on the DC-130A. This allowed me to do all the engine run maintenance and to train several others for engine run qualifications. This was the first time I was certified on this aircraft by a Standard Eval Pilot.

In March of 1976, I was given a line number to the next enlistment rank. I would sew on my new rank in June of 1976. My new commander, here in the 355th, had put me in for a promotion, and I was awarded a line number to E-5.

Military Service or Civilian Life

My four-year enlistment was coming to a decision. Was I to reenlist for another four years or to get out and try again at civilian life. The time in the service was ending. I had to start thinking about what my future was going to be. I had accomplished the reason why I re-entered military service: to mature.

It was not an easy decision for me. Pam was supposed to be with me and help make this decision. And, still in the back of my mind, I hung onto Pam as if she would call me, and we get back together. But with Pam's stubborn streak, I was sure she was gone and gone out of my life, even though she was not out of mine.

In June, I visited the Central Base Personnel Office (CBPO). I requested two options: An overseas tour in Germany for three years and flight engineer school for C-130s.

While at CBPO, someone looked up my records and saw that I had over 120 days of leave time to take. When Pam left, I never took any allotted vacation days per year; there was no reason to!

I stood at the edge of deciding not to reenlist for another four years, a decision looming as most of my unit's members were departing after completing eight years of service. Despite my deep affection for the Air Force- the hands-on work with aircraft, the pervasive scent of JP-4 fumes lingering from the engines, and the camaraderie- I found myself drawn to a new path. During my active duty, I delved into computer programming classes at Pima Community College, relishing the time spent learning. This starkly contrasted with my high school experience. Pursuing education or continuing in service weighed heavily in my decision, perhaps risking another failed relationship. Despite my certainty that I wouldn't marry, my heart remained steadfastly tethered to Pam, even in her absence of nearly three years.

I was not even out of CBPO when I decided not to reenlist. I walked back to cancel my request for flight engineers' school. I would be leaving active duty.

Then they informed me that I could not sell all my leave because I had over 120 days. They would not pay for more than sixty days of leave. My discharge date was calculated to be August 28, 1976. That coincided with my actual enlistment date back in 1968. My original discharge date should have been October 9th, 1976. But because they would pay me the leave I accrued and counting backward the number of days I had left after taking those days so as not to lose them, it brought my release date to the 28th of August 1976. The balance of my leave paid out to me would take me out to October 9th, 1976.

I was told that to avoid losing those days, I would have to begin my leave before I left CBPO. CBPO processed my leave paperwork, and I walked it over to the section chief, handed it to him, and said my goodbyes.

The following day, I got up as if I were in a different life, not having to report to the base. No more formations, no more unwanted TDYs, no more late-night engine runs, and no more nightmares without Pam.

I began looking for a job while on leave. I was hired and started work at Sears in credit collections. This was ironic as when Pam had left me, I spent a lot of time with credit collections on those things we bought together when we first arrived. Life was getting better. I was still on active duty and receiving my military and weekly pay from Sears. I attended Pima Community College and signed up for computer science programming in August. While signing up for classes, I also signed up for my VA education benefit of four hundred dollars a month. Life kept on getting better.

As evening settled in, the shrill tone of the telephone pierced the calm of my apartment. Initially reluctant to answer, my mind fixed on plans to grab a bite to eat. Yet, curiosity pulled me toward the ringing phone. *'Hello, do you know who this is?'* a familiar voice inquired from the other end. That of a person I love and I still do. I said, *'Yes,'* Pam. Despite my initial hesitation, I agreed to converse. Our discussion stretched for an hour, each minute tallying the cost of a long-distance call. Then the bombshell dropped, the man she ran off with was gone. She told me of his infidelities to her.

I had to hold back my thoughts as she continued her story. But those thoughts I could reveal were, you listen to someone tell you what was not true of me, and yet you ran off with this guy. Then, she casually mentioned that she had a son with him, which caught me off guard. If only my mind could talk and what it was thinking could tell her. Conflicting emotions surged within me, a mix of disbelief, resentment, and anger. How could she start a family with that guy? He shirked his responsibilities while I tried to build a life with her. The disparity between our efforts and her having a son with him just gnawed at my mind. My internal thought was, where is my son?

I had a lot of mixed feelings while I spoke with her. But I am still in love with her three years later. And just when I thought I could have gotten over her, she called, and she was back in my head.

It was never my intention to go back home, ever! Even after her phone call, I was not planning to return to Massachusetts. But she was so ingrained in my head that I just had to see her and see if we could repatriate our relationship.

I was doing well on my own, going to college and working. And now I just received an offer to work with Mountain Bell.

I now have friends in and out of the military here in Tucson. In one of them, we attend classes at Pima Community College and shared rides to classes. We also went to U of A football games as friends.

My life took an old turn; I left for my childhood home and Pam. On October 25th, 1976, I rented a U-Haul rooftop and went to be back home near Pam. But it would be almost a year before we would see each other once I arrived home.

Leaving Tucson

I journey back to Massachusetts. Just before I left, a new job offer from Bell Telephone Company came in. It was for a line technician, a position I had applied for shortly after leaving the service. I wanted to stay in Tucson, but the offer was for a town outside Tucson. Most of the cities surrounding Tucson were small. I declined the offer, mainly because it was not in Tucson, but I had Pam on my mind and wanted to get home and see her.

Arriving back in Massachusetts, I did not contact Pam immediately. I went to the Foxboro Company in East Bridgewater and applied for a job. I recognized the HR office girl as a former girl from my high school. She was a member of the Drill Team and two years ahead of me in school. She came over to me and said *'hello.'* I said, *'Terry,'* and we spoke for a couple of minutes before she brought me into her office. She then took me out on a plant tour, and when she brought me back to her office, she offered me a job on the first shift in production.

I started my career on the production floor and worked my way into engineering as an aide. I stayed at Foxboro for several years, then moved on to another position in another company that paid more for the same type of work.

While still at Foxboro, I was still missing military life. I first tried to enlist in the Air Force Reserves, but they had no openings in my AFSC or any other AFSCs I could get into. From the Air Force, I went to the Army National Guard, where they had several openings in helicopter maintenance. I enlisted and obtained the rank of Specialist Class 5, senior helicopter technician, UH-1. I would train at the former Air Force base, Otis, on Cape Cod one weekend a month.

Second Chance at Love

Then it happened. One day, on my way to work at my new job in Brockton, I stopped at a donut shoppe. I was always leaving for work early enough to have time to stop for a coffee and donut. It was sometime in September 1977, after the local schools were in session. Three school buses pulled into the Donut Shoppe parking area. While sitting at the counter, having my coffee and donut, I saw three women exit each school bus and walk towards the entrance. As I looked at who approached the shoppe, I noticed two women were older than the one. I watched all three women walk towards the shoppe.

As I continued to watch them come closer, one looked like Pam. How could that be? Pam driving a bus, I thought. Pam is a small, petite woman; the buses are so big. Besides, I hadn't seen Pam in over three years, and when we last spoke, I wasn't sure if she would still be single or detached from that man she had run off with. But I continued to watch all three as they entered. I could not believe it, that was Pam. Pam is still as beautiful as she was when she left me in Tucson. She hasn't aged at all. And still as thin as a rail. And having two children hasn't enlarged her breasts any. That's Pam! I'm sure!

Seeing her look my way, they all stopped inside the outer door. Did Pam see me sitting here? Are they going to leave now that she has seen me? Their hesitation lasted only about forty seconds before they continued into the store.

Pam left the group, walked over to where I was sitting, and approached me. *'Is it okay to talk, Bob?'* she asks. *'Sure,'* I say back to her. And then she walked closer to me and soon stood before me.

Entangled Hearts

She is looking right at me. I wonder if she is as surprised as I am? I wanted her even more now than I did in Arizona. Pam, my high school love. She never realized how much of a passion I had for her.

She asks if she can sit next to me, and I ask her to sit, as she used to do to me when we worked at D'Amatos. She tells me she wasn't sure if I would be pleasant to her or full of anger when I saw her. She must remember my anger when she walked away from me after signing the house papers. I was okay with her being here and near me. I wanted to reach out and hold her, to bring her in tightly so I could smell the scent of Pam once again.

Seeing her now brought back so many precious memories, and I was unsure how to respond to her as she sat next to me. My mind was working so fast with thoughts. Should I be angry with her? Should I not speak to her? Or should I just get up and silently walk out, saying nothing? Or throw her up on the counter and make sweet, passionate love. I knew only one thing now: I had never stopped loving her. Now that she was beside me, I never lost my love for her.

I did none of those things I had in my head, and we did talk. She gave me her telephone number and asked me to call her in the evening. Later that night, I called her and made a date with her for the upcoming Friday.

Friday evening arrived, and I drove over to her apartment. When I arrived, I exited my car and stood in front of this three-story house, wondering why. Why did she walk away from a home that she could have had? I walked up the steps to the stairs to get to her apartment. I was nervous as I climbed each step. And with each step, I wondered if a surprise would be waiting inside for me. A surprise of the man she ran off with just waiting. Never thinking that her two children would be in there, just the creep that stole her from me.

I reached the third-floor flat. As I was ready to knock on her door, I continued to think if what I was doing was right. I'm still in love with her and do not want to find out that she was no longer in love with me.

I knock on the door, and she answers and asks me in. Finding her in this apartment was disheartening, considering we bought a house together in Tucson. As I entered, I paused at the doorway, surveying the space to check if she was alone. Then came her voice, asking, 'Are you coming in?' I chuckled and proceeded inside. While we exchanged pleasantries and commented on the apartment's charm, my mind couldn't help but contrast it with the beautiful home we never got to share in Tucson. Still, I couldn't deny the nostalgia of seeing how she had arranged things here, reminiscent of our first apartment in Tucson.

She was not ready and needed a few more minutes. A lot of small talk happened between us until she came out of her bedroom ready for our date. She was just a vision of loveliness when she exited the bedroom. She was the Pam I fell in love with back at D'Amato's. And she was the girl I took out with me to Tucson to have for the rest of my life.

If she had stayed with me in Tucson, we could have moved back home and purchased a house with the money from the home sale.

She was the only one in the apartment this evening. She had taken her kids to her parents for the evening. I wondered what her parents would have thought had they known she was going out with me? Did she tell them? Most likely, she would have told her mother.

I should have felt vindictive toward her, but I did not. Sitting next to each other, it felt good to be beside her. I kept thinking of the past when she stood in the doorway of our apartment in Tucson and walked away.

Pam and I returned to her apartment, our hearts filled with deep affection. I was enamored with her, and as we settled into the cozy living room, our conversation flowed naturally, punctuated by moments of longing glances and sweet smiles. The atmosphere between us was changed with desire.

Our lips met, and a gentle exchange of kisses carried us into a more intimate space. From there, we found our way to the bedroom, where our bodies reconnected as if they had been yearning for each other all along. Her enchanting brown eyes radiated warmth and beckoned me closer. At the same time, her skin felt as soft and inviting as the finest silk. The tender nibbles at my ears sent shivers down my spine.

Our love making was an exquisite blend of passion and tenderness, infused with a hint of bashfulness that made it all the more exciting. Afterward, we lay in each other's arms, sharing laughter and intimate secrets. She confided in me about a unique experience after her second child, with a touch of humor in her voice. She had always been self-conscious about her breasts, but I assured her that, to me, they were nothing short of perfection.

We dove into a conversation about our shared history, reminiscing about the good times while gracefully avoiding the painful subjects that had long gnawed at my soul: who had spread the malicious rumor that I had been unfaithful to her.

I stumbled upon an unsettling revelation when I heard that a former neighbor had falsely informed Pam that I was being unfaithful. I had experienced a near-death encounter involving a Snickerdoodle with peanut butter. With a heavy heart, I comforted her, exclaiming, '*You left me for a mere rumor.*'

Reluctantly, I disclosed the details of my harrowing ordeal. As she inquired about my early return home, I relayed what little information

I had garnered from the Red Cross. Circumstances, our time together was filled with cherished moments. I reveled in the warmth of her embrace and the tender moments we shared, savoring both our physical intimacy and heartfelt conversations. I was resolute in my desire for our connection to endure.

Our evenings were often spent in each other's company, and I relished the moments when Pam and I were entwined. Our dates led us back to her apartment, where her two children would be under the care of her parents, affording us precious moments of privacy and connection.

Then, one evening, after we had made love, Pam brought up a teacher she knew in a private school she drove students to. She said he would leave the area for a new position in New Hampshire. How and why is she bringing this up to me? Wait a minute, I thought she wanted to be with me? Was I wrong?

I began to think, is this Tucson all over again? I wanted to be with her, but did she want to be with me? If so, why then this other guy?

The conversation has hit me hard. Stirring a whirlwind of emotions and memories. The mention of this man has ignited a storm of questions within me. Casting shadows of doubt on where my heart stands in her heart. My desire to be with her clashes with uncertainty with her mentioning this other guy.

The echoes of Tucson haunt me, almost like a haunting melody playing in the background of my thoughts. We had just shared some of the most vivid moments. Then, my mind returned to the apartment doorway she walked out of, and the day of the closing on the house in Tucson flickered in my mind's eye. Overlaid with a new image of her with someone else.

With us just lying here, our two bodies intimately entwined with one another. Yet, as if the past and present converge, thoughts blur the lines between reality and haunting memories. At that moment, post-love heightened my introspection, making me question the current dynamics of what our relationship was going to be?

Watching her sleep might have been comforting and disconcerting. Still, it was an intimate closeness that contrasted starkly with my emotional distance. These conflicting emotions were why I likely stirred a storm of hesitation in my mind about us being together again. This left me feeling adrift and unsure of what might be ahead of a renewed relationship.

Later, during our reconnection, thoughts of her parents came to mind. Are her parents wondering why I am back in your life? Did she regret her leaving me back then? Does she love me? Or would it just be a big mistake I would make again? Am I competing against this other man, and if we get back together and she does not like her decision, will she leave me again? Was Pam worth another trip down through hell? While holding each other, was she thinking of what she had just told me?

One evening, we were together, and more thoughts caused me to remain awake. A strange feeling was arousing me, and I decided to leave.

Pam woke up and asked what was happening; I created an excuse for why I was awake and would be leaving. I could sense that Pam knew I was lying, and she accepted it. With our final kiss, I left.

I made mistakes with Pam, no doubt. Refusing to compromise my self-worth, I choose not to surrender myself to her, only for her to depart, opting for another man instead of me.

When I left her that morning without talking with her about all the thoughts I had in my head, I regretted doing so. I was remorseful about it for many years. I loved her. I'd been in love with her since our meeting at

D'Amatos and the entire time she left. But I could not bring myself back into her life with the mentioning this other man. Why did she tell me about this other guy? Was she torn between us? Did she love me more?

I would never be able to survive her leaving me again. Nor did I ever want to experience that feeling of profound loneliness. All those thoughts went through my head as I walked out and away from her and to my car. Before I got to my car, I turned towards the apartment and looked up at the window from where I had just left. I wondered if she was sad about my departure...

I knew that would be my last time with her, and I would never return. I wanted to run back to her. As I stood in the driveway, I turned to run up those stairs into her apartment and tell her how much I loved her. I never wanted to let her go. But I was scared that she would walk away from me again.

Love Dilemma Again

Days later, I received a call at work from the man Pam had mentioned. It didn't register then, but how did he know where I worked?

His persistent calls echoed the events of August 1973. In one conversation, he asked about my feelings for Pam. Love for her was undeniable, yet fear loomed large. Why had she involved him in this situation?

During his second call, he assured me he wouldn't disrupt our relationship if my love for her was true. But shouldn't this conversation be about where he stands in her life and not him asking me? Did she reciprocate? Thoughts of Tucson flooded my mind, reminiscent of the painful memories from when Pam left with someone else in 1973.

History seemed to be repeating itself. The calls triggered past anguish. Despite the man's interest in my feelings for her, he couldn't grasp the devastation of her previous departure. It boiled down to my decision. Should I confront her? Was she orchestrating this? Having him call me instead of her asking me these questions.

Was I risking another heartbreak? And was the risk with her worth any more pain? Would this man persist in her life if we reconciled? What about our future together?

A final decision loomed, urging an immediate response. For days after his calls, I had done nothing but think of her and wanted to call her, but those other thoughts of her not committing to me would resurface. Was she worth the chance? I'm in a toxic, forbidden love. I love her so much that I hurt inside.

'*No*' was the answer I gave him on the phone, and then I hung up. I love her. I carry a passion for her. For years after I said, '*no*,' she was still in my mind.

My decision was hasty and wrong; I realized several months later that because of a farm, that would become an opportunity for me. But I told him he could have her.

I should have approached Pam and gotten all my answers from her before I gave him my answer. I needed answers from her, her parents, and how her reentering my life would be. What about her children? How would they think of us being together? And does this man calling me, just how does he fit into her life? And the man you ran off with, three years earlier, where does he fit into our relationship? As they share a child. Would she be willing to bear more children with me? I just should have been talking to Pam, but I just pushed her out and into the arms of another man.

I was also in the National Guard and wondered how that may affect our relationship. Would she have stayed with me? Or would she have a problem with my being in the military?

The Farm

After eighteen months in the Army National Guard, the Air Force Reserves finally called with a slot for me to join. They said they had a position available in Aerial Port AFSC (Air Force Specialty Code). If I wanted to return, I could be placed in that slot. I liked working on helicopters, but I liked Air Force life much more. I transferred from the Massachusetts Army National Guard to the Air Force Reserves.

With this transfer came a new location for my training assemblies: Westfield, Massachusetts. After one of my Air Force UTAs (unit training assemblies), I decided to find a family member. A great aunt and uncle live in the area. I knew of the towne they moved to, and with that information, I headed out on my quest to find them and the farm we were to move to some sixteen years earlier.

After driving for several hours from Westfield and up this mountain, I came to the towne of Middlefield. I decided to take a moment and soak in the quaint charm of the general store, where I happened to stop to inquire the name of my great-uncle.

Middlefield, a snapshot of nostalgia, with a wooden walkway leading up to its entrance and a single gas pump standing sentinel out front. Inside, it felt like I stepped back into the pages of an old New England novel. A group of seasoned gentlemen, their faces etched with the stories of the years gone by, were engrossed in a game of checkers. They puffed leisurely on pipes and shared tales that seemed as ancient as the store itself.

With a hopeful tone in my voice, I inquired among these gentlemen if they knew of a man by the name of Clayton Crothers. To my surprise, their initial reaction was laughter. I couldn't fathom what could be so amusing about my question. Perplexed but undeterred, I approached the weathered wooden counter, where an older man now stood, holding on to his Sunday paper and looking small and frail.

The man behind the counter gazed at me curiously and asked, '*Who might you be young one?*' I introduced myself and mentioned my father's name. '*I am the son of Kenneth A. Crothers*,' I said to him. At that moment, a recognition ignited the older gentleman's eyes as he stood at the counter with the newspaper in hand. It dawned on him that I was his family, a connection he had not seen in over sixteen years and had not anticipated ever seeing another family member from the Southeastern area of Massachusetts.

From that point on, our meeting took a heartwarming turn. My great-uncle Clayton, now with the weight of years upon him, invited me to accompany him back to his home. I readily agreed, eager to bridge the gap of time and distance that had separated us for so long. As we made our way to his residence, memories of my great-aunt Helen flooded back. She had always been the epitome of warmth and charm during our visits to their grand mansion at what we knew as kids 303 Maple Street.

Little did I know that this unexpected reunion would not only rekindle family ties but also lead to a flood of cherished memories, making it a journey back in time to when I was just a child, visiting this enchanting corner of New England with my father.

Nestled amidst the undulating hills of the Berkshires, Middlefield boasts a history as rich and vibrant as the landscape enveloping it. My great aunt and uncle were heading into retirement when they sold their home in Springfield and purchased this farm in the hills of the Berkshires.

Their farm was an easy drive from my unit training facility, Westover. Here lies the picturesque farm that became the tranquil haven for my great aunt and uncle. This idyllic towne, once a bustling thoroughfare during the eight-teen-hundreds for the stagecoach route from Springfield to Pittsfield, held their new home in its embrace.

The home adjacent to their farm was the stagecoach stop, standing stoically across the road. Here, amidst the verdant surroundings, horses would leisurely rest and rejuvenate before embarking on their journey downhill toward the vibrant city of Pittsfield... This location served as more than a stop; it was a nexus of connection, where the rhythm of rural life intersected with the transient hustle and bustle of travelers enroute to Pittsfield.

Middlefield, steeped in history, with its rolling hills adorned by lush foliage, painted a canvas of serene beauty. Each season infused the landscape with its own charm-from the vibrant hues of autumn foliage to the snow-blanketed tranquility of winter and the blossoming exuberance of spring. The towne bore witness to the passage of time yet retained an enduring allure and unspoken testament to the harmonious coexistence of nature and history within its fold.

The farmhouse, situated mostly on thirty-five acres of wooded land, was built in 1878 by a Civil War Veteran. He used the bonus money he was promised from the State of Massachusetts when he enlisted in the Army during the Civil War.

The farm had two barns, becoming known as the big and small barns. The smaller barn had a greenhouse attached to it where my great-uncle grew plants and experimented with hydroponics. He was an award-winning grower of roses and sure liked experimenting with other ways to grow plants. In front of the greenhouse, he had a cold cellar where he would start seedlings for planting in the spring.

The larger barn had four horse stalls, and in the front of the barn were caretakers' quarters. Now owning his farm, he relished stories of his days on the Vermont farm where he and his brothers grew up.

The main house, built in 1878, had three large bedrooms and a bathroom on the home's second story. Underneath them was the central part of the house with the family room and a vast fieldstone fireplace. The family room ran the entire with of the house. The other side of the main house had a library in the front, and behind it was what they called the birthing room, which also was the dining room. There was no kitchen in the original portion of the house until 1938. That was when the second addition was added to the main house.

Between those two rooms on the first floor was a lovely hallway and grand stairway that took you to the second-floor bedrooms. The two front bedrooms faced the Northwest, with dormers that had double windows in them. At the top of the stairs to the bedrooms was a sitting area where you could sit, along with a small writing desk in front of the windows. Two bedrooms were accessible from the top of the stairs, while the third had a small hallway to enter the bedroom.

The newer edition built onto the main portion of the home is where a sizeable in-door kitchen was, and a second set of stairs was made to access the second floor. Four more bedrooms were added to this addition, as were two more bathrooms.

The house was built on a stone wall foundation using the rocks from the five acres that were cleared for either growing or pasture for the horses.

Around the property were apple trees, blueberry bushes, and grape vines, which lined the front of the property along with the main road coming up from Springfield. The side of the property was pretty open.

Other than the five-acre cleared, the rest of the farm was all wooded land. And within the middle of all those trees was a lone artesian well. That is where the water to the house came from.

In 1963, my parents were asked to move to the farm. My dad's uncle wanted us to help develop a business using the endless water flow of the artesian well. There was all kinds of talk going around in our home about living on the farm and the lifestyle we would have. I was about to enter high school when this was to take place. But what was not known to me was a falling out in the family between my dad and his uncle, which stopped that move, and we stayed in Abington.

Grown up now, some twenty-five years after 1963, my great-uncle invited me to stay on the farm for one weekend. He educated me about the farm owner he had purchased it from and told me she was a widow and had lost her husband on the Titanic.

Standing in the vicinity of the barns, one is greeted by a captivating and everchanging view that evolves with the progression of October. The farm, nestled on the rolling landscape, offers a picturesque vista of the surrounding valley.

As you gaze out over the valley, the first thing that strikes you is the mesmerizing transformation of the foliage. The month of October ushers in the autumnal spectacle with trees adorned in vibrant hues of crimson, gold, and amber. The leaves have begun their gradual descent, creating a breathtaking tapestry of colors that seems to intensify with each passing day.

Throughout the month, the weather plays a pivotal role in shaping the view. At times, low-hanging clouds drift lazily through the valley, shrouding the landscape in a soft, misty veil. It creates a dreamlike atmosphere, making the farm appear as though it's perched above the clouds, as if it were in its own tranquil world, untouched by the hustle and bustle below.

Standing proudly amidst this scenic beauty, the weathered barns exude an aura of rustic charm and industry, a testament to the generations of farmers who have toiled land here, cultivating the fertile land and nurturing the agricultural heritage of this region.

In this serene and ever-evolving panorama, one can't help but be enchanted by the beauty of nature's seasonal ballet. The view from the area near the barns encapsulates the essence of October on the farm, where the interplay of foliage and weather creates a landscape that is both dynamic and enchanting, a testament to the timeless beauty of rural life.

After spending several months visiting the farm, I received a heartfelt invitation to make it my permanent residence. They inquired whether I would be willing to assist in its upkeep. I embraced the opportunity without hesitation and moved in on a crisp October day in 1978. Little did I know that great uncle Clayton had more surprises for me.

He confided that he and my great-aunt Helen wished to pass the farm down to me upon his passing, with a few conditions. I would need to purchase the farm for the sum of thirty thousand dollars and ensure that my dear great-aunt continued to reside there for the rest of her days. Given her pleasant disposition, I readily accepted the terms. I initiated the process of acquiring the farm at the agreed-upon price.

My days were filled with employment as an Industrial Engineer Aide at a nearby factory, making the daily commute from the farm to Springfield and back. On my UTA (Unit Training Assembly) weekends, I would return to the farm at night, eliminating the need for base lodging. Life at that moment seemed exceptionally fulfilling.

Upon returning from a reserve weekend, my great-uncle awaited me to enter the kitchen. He had something of importance to discuss with me. He had been thinking of bottling the artesian well water from the farm and selling it. This all sounded good to me, except for the bottled water.

I asked him how and who would buy bottled water when they get water from the home faucet! He stated that the water on the farm was from an artesian well. And it was better quality water than from poorly run and controlled water treatment plants in most cities. I agreed with him but knew I could not do it alone.

With the option to purchase the farm, I thought my brother and his family would like to move here. The house was large enough for both families to live in should I pursue Pam and ask her to join me in living up on this farm and for us to marry. I would use my VA to purchase the farm and live under the rules of my great-uncle for the time he was alive.

My brother and his family came up for an overnight, and he and I walked the land and its woods. That night, my brother and his wife discussed it and decided not to move up and live on the farm. At first, I was devastated, but I understood.

The Finding of Pam

I thought of returning and finding Pam and hoping she was still unattached. I was excited about this farm and wanted to tell her about the farm and have her move to be with me. She had been on my mind for several months. Now that I live in western Massachusetts, togetherness may be what I need.

I found myself hastily passing judgment on letting Pam venture into the embrace of another man. Uncertainty loomed large as I grappled with the weight of our shared history in Tucson, not to mention our recent shared experiences. The question that tormented my mind was whether I should seek her out, urging her to relocate to the farm and build a new life with me. Doubts crowded my thoughts. Could I genuinely begin anew and cosign the past to oblivion? Yet, a persistent nagging fear lingered- what if I couldn't place my trust in her? Without trust, I would forever be haunted by the specter of potential rivals and the looming possibility of her departure. The farm, far more financially burdensome than our former home in Tucson, felt like a sacred commitment to upholding a promise to my great-uncle that I couldn't forsake.

Entangled Hearts

FROM THE BOB CROTHERS COLLECTION-Skyline Farms 1978

The large red barn had a second level for hay storage. Behind the large barn are five clear acres for horses to graze or become a planting field.

FROM THE BOB CROTHERS COLLECTION-Julie 1978 @ Skyline Farms

A U-shaped driveway brought you to the farm from the main road. The farm was bordered by a fence in the front.

An old water tower stood just behind the greenhouse, which stored the water to the house from the well down below it in the days before electricity. I considered using the second floor in this smaller barn as an artist's studio.

FROM THE BOB CROTHERS COLLECTION-Small barn & greenhouse

There was a school in the town that Pam's two sons would attend up to the sixth grade. From there, they would have had to be bussed to Pittsfield to finish their education. Middlefield has a general store and a church.

The one thing I missed was a church, and this town has one. I knew I needed religion in my life if I wanted Pam back.

Entangled Hearts

FROM THE BOB CROTHERS COLLECTION-Church in Middletown 1978

One Sunday morning, I left the farm early and drove to Pam's old apartment, only to discover she had moved. With an unwavering determination to locate her, I navigated towards her parent's house, where I had once been welcomed while we dated in high school. Then I made mistakes; I was to tenderly give her my affection of love for her in the form of a friendship ring, only to provide it to the road in a fit of anger. A fleeting thought crossed my mind: might that cherished ring have resurfaced unexpectedly after eleven years?

I sat along the side street for several minutes, reluctant to face her parents directly. I hoped to catch Pam if she happened to be visiting and answer the door herself, sparing me the awkward encounter with her parents. As the morning turned into noon, I mustered the courage to approach their house and seek information about Pam's whereabouts. Nervous but driven by my love for her, I parked in front of her parents' home.

Approaching the front door, I barely had a chance to knock before her mother opened it, her face registering a mixture of surprise and nostalgia. In the background, I could hear her father, clearly upset by my presence. He ordered his wife to close the door with a shout directed at me. As I peeked around the door, I hadn't expected them to provide Pam's location, but the anger in her father's eyes spoke volumes. It was enough to make me realize I had overstayed my unwelcome.

I pleaded fervently with her mother to disclose Pam's whereabouts, desperate to bridge the chasm that had separated us. But her mother insisted on my departure, firmly supported by her father's resolute stance. The door slammed shut, severing the last strand connecting me to her.

Standing there, Pam, the love of my life, had slipped away, leaving an abyss of emptiness. Reluctantly, I turned away, each step carrying the weight of memories and an unspoken plea for her mother to relent to reveal her daughter's location. But it never happened. Each backward glance pierced my soul with fragments of cherished times from our past and recently. I yearned to rewind the clock to 1966 and rewrite our story.

Upon my return to the farm, the decision not to purchase it became an emblem of the life I was leaving behind. I departed, settling briefly in a small studio apartment in Westfield, grappling with the uncertainty of my future without her.

Within a month, I relinquished my job, completed my reserve duty, transitioned to inactive status, and withdrew my college application, all efforts to escape the haunting echoes of a life intertwined with hers.

The resolve to restart my life propelled me to Arizona, a distance I hoped would quell the echoes of her absence. She would never comprehend the depth of my love, how it surged upon hearing her voice say those words that evening…

'Do you know who this is?'

About the Author

Robert A. Crothers is an author with a penchant for storytelling, drawing inspiration from his own life experiences and military background. Born in Hanover and raised in Abington, Massachusetts, he has been crafting autobiographical fiction stories that expertly blur the lines between truth and imagination, memoir and satire.

Crothers' literary journey has been a tapestry of emotions, memories, and life-changing encounters. His writing has found its way into the pages of various magazines, where he shares gripping narratives of his military experiences and personal struggles. His candid approach to storytelling is characterized by a raw honesty that resonates deeply with readers.

His partner's sudden departure, just after they had purchased a home together, left him with a bewildering void. The book delves into the complexities of love and loss and their profound impact on one's life.

In 'From Tarmac to Skies: Stories about Crew Chiefs in Vietnam,' Crothers transports readers to the turbulent times of the Vietnam War, offering a glimpse into the experience of those who worked on the frontlines to keep aircraft operational. His narrative brings to life those unsung heroes' struggles, camaraderie, and heroism.

Robert A. Crothers' literary journey began with A US Airman's Experience in Vietnam: Unforgotten Memories of Service and Romance.' Published by iUniverse Publishing. This marked the genesis of his storytelling, setting the stage for his subsequent works.

Robert A. Crothers' books are rooted in real-life experiences, making his writing relatable and profoundly moving. Through his evocative storytelling, he invites readers on a journey of self-discovery, resilience, and the enduring human spirit. Robert A. Crothers' works offer a unique blend of reality and fiction, creating narratives that resonate with the heart and soul.